T0170153

INKLE AND YARICO

Being the narrative of Thomas Inkle
Concerning his shipwreck
and long sojourn among the Caribs,
his marriage to Yarico, a Carib woman
and his life on the island of Barbados

ALSO BY BERYL GILROY

Black Teacher, Bogle-L'Ouverture, 1976
Frangipani House, Heinemann, 1986
Boy Sandwich, Heinemann, 1989
Stedman and Joanna: A Love in Bondage, Vantage, 1991
Echoes and Voices (poetry), Vantage, 1991
Sunlight and Sweet Water, Peepal Tree Press, 1994
Gather the Faces, Peepal Tree Press, 1994
In Praise of Love and Children, Peepal Tree Press, 1994
Leaves in the Wind: Collected Writings, Mango Publishing, 1998
The Green Grass Tango, Peepal Tree Press, 2001

INKLE AND YARICO

BERYL GILROY

P E E P A L   T R E E

First published in Great Britain in 1996
Peepal Tree Press Ltd
17 King's Avenue
Leeds LS6 1QS
Reprinted 2015

ISBN 9780948833984

Supported by
ARTS COUNCIL
ENGLAND

In loving memory
P.E. Gilroy
1919-1975

CHAPTER ONE

As a young man of twenty, I welcomed the spring, that splendid time of the year. I was in love and had just been informed by my eldest brother, Jonathan, that my betrothal had been agreed and that, consequent upon my return from Barbados in the West Indies, my marriage would take place. The terms had been settled that very day, and my brother had been sent on ahead to acquaint me of them. True, the lady possessed a substantial fortune, but that was only a part of the matter. She was beautiful too. I tore open the letter which had accompanied Jonathan and found the details well set out by my father. My heart sang softly against my breast and my thoughts, like the opening buds about me, continued a gentle unfolding of dreams. My native land seemed greener than ever and I drank down the sweetness of the air as though it were strong ale.

My youth streamed ahead of me into the future. Of the three sons, I was the tallest, the strongest, the Adonis of the family, greatly petted by my mother and spoilt by my father. Jonathan had followed my father's footsteps into the mercantile word, importing and retailing artefacts and antiquities to discerning, as well as gullible customers. What he bought for a pittance in France and Italy, he made certain to sell dear at home. Adam, my second brother, had been apprenticed to a lawyer with chambers in Lincoln's Inn Fields, and I was left free to seek my fortune with destiny as my guide.

I had not been sent to school as my brothers were. After much consideration, my father encouraged two Huguenot gentlemen, who had fled to England from their French persecutors, to take charge of my education.

Mr Kaufman, at first stolid and unsmiling, was in fact a worthy man in the field of mathematics and literature. He encouraged me greatly to become a master of mathematics, a fact which delighted my father. He, on his occasional visits to the school-room in our house, would encouragingly say, 'Be a master of mathematics. Be concerned with advantage and avoid loss, for loss leads certainly to beggary. Always think to your advantage.'

Mr Koenig, tolerant and easy-going, a small, round-eyed man who reached up to my armpits, taught me languages with much solicitude for my state of mind. His hands, as he turned the pages of the books, were like two beautiful creatures that sought only to caress whatever they touched. He instilled in me both the love of all natural languages and the wonders of verse, and took pains to bestow upon me a small volume of Sanskrit poems which had come into his possession when he served the East India Company as a clerk.

In addition, I had two other teachers, but well concealed. They were the gamekeeper's sons and they assiduously taught me the arts of bare-knuckle fighting. After any such sly imbroglio, if I came off the worst, the elder would sneak a small gin cup to my lips and all would be merry and well. The younger lad, when merry, would forget his station and say, 'Master Tommy! You might be took for a maid with such a mass of golden thatch resting upon your shoulders! Men might even think it a periwig — your thatch!' I would bid him hold his tongue and remember his place.

That morning I stood upon the Downs in full view of the river with its many ships waiting to depart across the oceans and the seas. Trade was the blood of this country and there I stood waiting to play a part in it. During the Commonwealth period, when Cromwell ruled the kingdom, my great-grandfather had bought lands on the British island of Barbados, and upon it had settled indentured Irish malefactors and English miscreants who had fallen foul of the law. These lands had passed to my grandfather and then my father, but, despite the plentiful addition of African slaves, being badly managed by overseers and attorneys, the lands had not prospered but had moved steadily towards loss, which greatly aggrieved my papa.

I was therefore sent to take a full measure of affairs, and to acquaint myself with the reasons why these slaves, although housed and fed, had failed to work conscientiously. I was to report to my papa on these affairs, after my safe return to England, and with him dwell upon the steps we should take to obtain a satisfactory return upon our investments.

Alice Sawyer, my betrothed and heart's desire, had accompanied my family (Papa excepted) to see me off on my journey. Each one proceeded to give me stern warnings as to the climate and the vagaries of life in such uncivilised parts. Alice alone raised my spirits. With the full flavour of her love for me candid in her eyes, she whispered, 'Mind you get there safely, Tommy; for my dearest wish is that you wed me, one year this day.'

'And what if the seas should engulf me?' I asked.

'Then I shall pluck you from their very depths.' She laughed softly. We told each other of all our dreams and hopes, although not a word was spoken. Looks and sighs and subtle touches conveyed every loving message. I was greatly put out that my father had not come to bid me adieu, for his good opinion gave me much courage and pleasure; but my mother assured me that urgent business with the Duke of Marchmont had compelled his absence.

My father was an extremely versatile man. He had often taken me to the 'House of Lords', a club which met each week at the Three Herrings, an ale house in the Chancery Lane. There he held discourses with men who dealt in trade of all kinds — captains of sloops, ships, frigates and merchantmen, and characters who delighted in knavery. Like the other members, my father paid a shilling a week, absent or present, for the upkeep of his club. There were many rooms, all occupied. I knew that from the way his cronies clamoured out from the innermost recesses of the House of Lords for ale; and sometimes, when I wandered outside to spy upon the pot-boy's antics, it was not unusual to discover highwaymen, immaculately dressed as gentlemen of the road, kissing their molls adieu before setting off to feather their nests.

The members of the House of Lords were in awe of my father, who was a learned man, full of sayings, quotations, roguery and proverbs. I would have liked him to witness my departure but he could not and, sad at heart, I bade farewell to all ashore and with my sea-chest boarded the boat that would convey me to the sloop at anchor on the river.

I recognised Captain Sedgecombe, who was an intimate of my father's. He was a large man, muscular and imposing, with the impress of the sea and the wind in his eyes. From the way he explained the vagaries and individuality of his ship I could see that he loved her, although he seemed to be too big a man for her. He wore coarse breeches, a yellow waistcoat and a full buckled jacket, thick knitted stockings, a coarse yarn overcoat and heavy sea-boots, all giving bulk to his height.

The Achilles was a merchantman about four hundred tons burden, with two eight-pounders on each broadside. There were thirty sailors, the captain, his black boy, Jimmy, the bosun, the coxswain and myself. The ship was loaded with equipment and food for the plantations and carried no other passenger excepting myself, the captain having been per-suaded by my father to convey me to Barbados.

There was little variety in the routines of life on board. Each man had his duty and that being already understood, one got the impression of application and industry. Jimmy, though, was a diversion to the men. He loved the captain who had bought him for five pounds at Greenwich.

I was given a comfortable berth and spent a great deal of time reading and rereading my father's last letter to me. He had written:

'There are seven classes of mankind. The rich who live plentifully; the middle sort who live well; the working trades who labour hard but feel no want; the country folk who fare indifferently; the poor that toil hard, but do not suffer want; and the miserable who suffer want. Remember: you are of the first class.'

How irksome! I knew only too well where I belonged.

The early part of the voyage passed without great event until, as we approached the harbour at Antwerp, where we were to drop anchor and take on board more cargo, a storm broke. Pale yellow streaks of lightning ran recklessly through the skies. The thunder, an angry animal, rumbled in the distance. The sea rose, whipped by thick sheets of rain. Out of the mist came a low, distant sound — plaintive and beseeching, as if yearning for every evil thing on earth to depart from it. Some of the sailors crossed themselves.

'A slaver!' another whispered. 'It's like a ghost ship, 'idin' itself in that mist.'

I noticed Jimmy looking extremely apprehensive. I tried to calm the fellow, but avoiding my hand, he shrieked until the captain threatened to leather him.

As we journeyed on, the colour of the water changed, indicating that we had come into what all Englishmen designated as foreign parts. The skies showed more subtle and less determined hues than English skies. No other ship passed us although we expected to see numbers on this leg of the triangular route.

The captain continually swept the sea and the sky with his telescope, noticing every shift in the wind. After five weeks we entered the tropics. The weather had become noticeably hotter. Occasionally, colourful tropical birds passed overhead, their plumage like Joseph's coat that excited his brothers' envy. Suddenly the wind died on us and there we sat becalmed, the tropic heat all around us. The sea became a glimmering sheet, the wind gently tickling its face. Not a cloud sullied the blue of the sky.

At night the stars came out in quantity and the wind blew colder. By dawn on the fifth day there was a shift in the wind and Mother Carey's chickens appeared, auguring a storm, and flying like a shower of pebbles over our bows. We could hear the wind moaning in the distance, as if in mortal pain.

'Where are we now, Cap'n?' I asked.

'Not far from the island of Jamaica. God keep us. Smugglers infest these murderous waters.'

By dawn the wind came steady and, with sails unfurled, we began to make good headway. Then buildings came into view, some decrepit and unkempt against the shoreline, and a swarm of ships of a variety of shapes and sizes. Kingston, a bristling place where the flotsam of humanity had taken refuge, was like a cauldron on the boil. Jimmy, glad to be able to use his land-legs, took me thereabouts, his eyes rambling over every place he came upon.

As I walked among the citizens, my own people were evidently struck by my appearance. Not a few women turned to give me warm and friendly glances, but I thought about my beloved Alice and kept myself pure in that place. Jimmy, though, disappeared from my side, telling me he would make his own way back to the ship. On my own, and in receipt of constant solicitations, I was quite relieved to return to *The Achilles, to* raise anchor and put to sea again.

We had been sailing for hours when we became aware of a huge silence on the ship. Everybody seemed to have realised the dreadful occurrence at the same time.

'Good God! Jimmy! Jimmy has been missed!' the captain bellowed through the silence.

'We will have to go back!' yelled Jock.

'No good going back again. We will pick him up on our return,' the captain decided after some thought.

'What will he do?' I wondered. I was certain, though, that someone would take him in.

We ploughed on through an incomprehensible sea for another day. It was as if deep down in the entrails of the ocean, a bubbling and boiling was taking place, throwing up a mist that obscured the sunshine that was usually so fierce and clear in these parts. This mist was quite unlike the gossamer haze that hung upon the morning air in my beloved England. This mist was opaque and substantial, with the appearance of syrup thickly spread. It served its purpose which was to cause us perplexity over its mysterious quality.

By and by, the sky began to clear a little, but one particular spot in the distant heavens was darkest of all, as if concentrating evil in that place. It appeared to twist itself into a spiral, each moment gaining strength by its own contortions and moving rapidly here and there with the ferocity of a tiger. The moaning flowed out in an increasing stream from some secret place and mingled with the very flesh, blood and bones of the wind. It raced towards us, uncoiling as it came.

As we hastened to secure all the now sodden equipment, our voices were lost in that blend of terror raised by the elements. The sea, at that moment mountainous and foaming single-mindedly, tore us along, advancing, receding and ripping parts of our ship away. In less than an hour our guns and most of our cargo had disappeared. The sea had us at its mercy, its colossal force turning and tumbling us about as driftwood. The helmsman tried to steer the boat into the waves and ride them like a sea-bird, but alas! the wind turned us about again and, in full control, the sea took us towards shallower water, to hurl us into an unknown place. I began to swim, not caring where I went, yet asking the hand of fate to lead me towards *terra firma*. But the waves were so strong that swimming was impossible, so I could only lie upon their backs at the mercy of their cruel play. When at last I did come to rest, I felt a monstrous tiredness, like a man who had been whipped as I lay prone among debris from trees and other wreckage. Fearfully I waited for what seemed an eternity before I called out to my companions. To my joy, the captain hollered back.

'There is twelve of us left alive 'ere. God save our souls and yours. Everything is gone, Master Tommy. We just 'ave what is left of our lives.'

I slipped along the shore into a cove where the others were gathered and lay down on the sand to rest myself.

'What would I not give for a drop of ole Adam's ale,' said Noah. 'Let us seek water!'

'There may be savages lurking in them trees to 'ack us to death,' said Adam.

'Seek out footprints then.'

They wandered about seeking footprints and in the process leaving their own. Apart from the trees knocked down by the force of the hurricane, the heap of vines entangled on the sand and the general maiming of Nature, all was green and peaceful, but as each hour passed it brought greater hunger. Noah, who had lost his shirt, had been so blistered by the heat of the sun that his back seemed a large red sore. The men fell to eating clams and seaweed which aggravated their thirst. At last, the sun began to sink, the wind became a breeze, chilly from the heavy vapour contained in it, and we nestled into the sand and went to sleep. I was in great pain and could lie only on my front, sleep coming upon me in no other way.

When I awoke, I found that, save for the captain, I was alone. He told me that the men had set off to gather fruit, which was numerous upon the ground. I thought to follow, but as they were out of sight, I thought it best to await their return.

Suddenly a most devilish cry sliced the air and the men emerged from the trees running for their lives and calling upon God to save them from certain death. I scuttled along the sand, hiding in the boscage that bordered the beach as best I could, but the thud of wood on flesh and bone assailed my ears. Intermingling with that heinous sound were the voices of the men beseeching their attackers to spare their lives. But the bloodlust of the natives who had ambushed my companions had to be satiated. Their pleadings continued until mercifully silenced by death. The creatures now turned their attention to the captain who, being slower in flight, was still exposed on the sand. Hastily rushing out into the water, he decided to take his chance with the elements but the savages swam out after him, yelling with frustration at his flight. 'Oh God,' I prayed. 'Shield me! Protect me.' Hardly daring to move further, I waited until all I could hear were the cries of sea-birds wheeling above me and the sound of surf breaking on the sand. The heat burnt my body like flaming cinders, leaving me in the grip of a mighty thirst. Though generally no friend to darkness, I prayed for it now. I needed a safe, encircling blackness to conceal myself, and at that moment envied the savage natives the colour of their skins. Half-dead for lack of water, I waited for twilight to come, and then, skirting the sand and tufts of grass, I crept with great trepidation towards a little clump of trees which provided me with welcome shelter. Even at that moment I expected to see a satanic shadow above me, menacing me with club or spear. With the captain gone, the men hacked to eternity, and me alone upon this island of death, I felt a mangling of my will to live. Oh, the horror of being forgotten on the island!

I wanted to shout for help, but I controlled those instincts. Even at my distance from the slaughter I could not fail to notice the boxlike head of these savages, and the thought of falling into their hands made my blood freeze even in the heat. Darkness fell abruptly, almost angrily, but at last I felt some slight protection. I was alone on a dangerous island within close proximity of savages. I had seen intrepid and determined Captain Sedgecombe depart into the womb of the sea. My Bible, containing my father's last letter to me, had been lost, but my book of poems, though sodden, had been dried by the heat and held together. Apart from my water-stained silk shirt and breeches, my shoes devoid of buckles, my stockings mercifully quite whole, and my little book in its leather container, I possessed nothing in the world. From that moment my book became a treasure. My parents had equipped me with the qualities of hope and endurance, and so, casting my fate upon my Creator, I took heart and again fell asleep on the sand.

When the sound of the new day intruded upon me, my first thought was to flee the dismal scene of my companions' slaughter. I was led by the hand of God into a natural enclosure that could easily have been the lair of a ravenous animal. It was in fact a cave, made comfortable with mosses and leaves as though for an assignation. I crept further in and made myself as snug as prudence allowed. And so the hours passed.

At last, driven forth by my thirst, but still holding caution close, I walked down a rugged path and came upon a creek of clear cool water and, looking up, saw a maiden contentedly swimming naked in the water. She had not yet discovered my presence so I was able to observe the intimacy between herself and the water, glistening and lively around her. Rapt away, I enjoyed her splendid physique. She was buxom, above the middle height and well-proportioned, the first living, naked woman I had ever seen. I feasted my young eyes upon a truly surprising work of nature, voluptuous and yet tantalising at the same time. I looked unashamedly at her and was astonished that, though black, all her parts were as those in the pictures in the hands of the gamekeeper's lads.

Her hair, neatly curled, was fixed in a circlet around her head and showed some adulteration with the woollen hair of Africans. As she drew closer, I saw more of her body, which drew my eyes as gold to a lodestone.

Her only dress consisted of a small square apron of beads interwoven with shells, which, I learnt later, custom dictated always to be worn. Her figure was as perfect in detail as a European's, save for the little extravagance of flesh. In every other respect she was an Eve in Eden — two ripe apples for breasts, her waist shapely and inviting, her flesh young and firm.

About her there was a certain lack of finesse, an unfamiliarity with modesty as I knew it, and *that* most of all which set her apart in my mind as being of a civilisation inferior to my own. She was but Nature's child and appeared no more than eighteen years of age. As she clambered out of the creek, she glanced behind her as though she determined to avoid a surprise and then, smiling to herself, she proceeded down a narrow path, her buttocks round and curved and fleshy. After she had gone, I noticed a square of tortoise shell lying on the ground. I picked it up but had no time to scrutinise it, for I could see her returning. She systematically began looking for her trinket and the more fruitless the search, the more agitated and distressed she became.

The impulse to set her mind at ease swept over me and I stepped out in front of her and held out the object she was so obviously determined to find. With a tiny gasp she snatched it from me and her eyes became a mixture of terror and inquisitive surprise, her hands trembling a little. How could I convey my great longing for water to her? I pointed to the creek and mimed the act of drinking. Her uninhibited smile irked me, but she led me towards a tree aflame with flowers gushing out of the branches like water from a fountain. Jumping surprisingly high, she grasped a bunch of flowers, all the while muttering a Carib word which I was later to learn meant 'water-giver'. Deftly she squeezed the buds, which yielded up such an abundance of water I could do naught but thank my Redeemer for sending such an amiable child of nature to rescue me from certain death through the fangs of thirst. I motioned that I was hungry too and, escorting me back into the cave I had just vacated, she departed, but not before bidding me with a series of eloquent gestures to await her return to that same spot.

After she had gone I was invaded by feelings of suspicion. I was doubly a prisoner, first to the island and then to my doubts. I began to shiver as visions of the massacre of my comrades hounded me. I worried at one single thought: How could I turn this moment to my advantage? Could I trust the girl not to betray me? I waited in mingled hope and dread for her return.

She was alone when she came back after about an hour, bringing me fruit, fish and roots. I was so hungry I ate the food without a moment allowed for any other thought. I do not remember any of the food having a distinctive or unusual taste. I simply ate until satiated. She moved me to another place, a larger cave, and then she departed, leaving a barricade of brush and scrub to keep inquisitive animals away from me.

When next she came, I could see two aspects of ownership

most clearly displayed. She had found me as a child finds a treasure, a shell, a distinctive plant, a crab with an unusual claw upon the sand; therefore I belonged to her and, as her prisoner, she could do as she liked to my person. She sat stroking my hair and in no uncertain manner displayed her desire for me. She removed her apron and I discovered that beneath that she wore a shield, a triangle of split bark which protected her against unsolicited attention. It was I who needed help in such matters and by now felt truly sinful.

> 'She needeth no instruction in the art
> Of using woman's ways to win man's heart.
> The lily's scarlet stamens grew untaught,
> The bee came freely, wishing to be caught.'

Each day she returned, bringing me folded leaves containing messes of strange food. She delighted in my person, my height, my hairy body, which fascinated her, and in my manhood, to which she felt she had rightful claim. Her body, her head excepted, was free of hair, for in her tribe, I discovered, such hair was an encumbrance to the dyes used for protection. We had no words to make our intentions known but we spoke the language of the heart. She whispered her name into my ear as it was a forbidden thing in the tribe to utter one's name aloud.

'My name is Inkle,' I said. 'Repeat after me, "Inkle loves Yarico. Inkle loves me".'

She smiled and made the most amusing attempts at saying, 'Inkle loves me.'

I began to feel the need to exercise my long legs, but her gestures of warning prevented me. She was a young and passionate girl and enjoyed being a woman and functioning as one who had found an ideal, strange and obliging lover. She was completely without pretence. Our dark cave had become a den of unspoken delights. I taught her words of love and, in teaching her to say 'My love to you', I was compelled to say that too. It meant nothing to me or to her. She was pure instinct, for to survive in her world, to be at one with Nature's rhythms and to heed its customs, there was no place for thought and reason. She enjoyed me as a connoisseur enjoys a new taste. With deep wonder in her eyes she stroked and caressed the spoilt silk of my shirt and the fabric of my coarse stockings.

'Silk,' I whispered. 'I shall buy you a silken gown, pretty maid! I will take you to my country far across the sea and dress you in fine jewels.' Her eyes would shine at the sound of my voice, the flow of my words and the arrogance of my delivery. She was mine and I wholly hers, although from time to time Alice intruded upon my thoughts, and left me with a sense of unease and shame.

The cave was my safety but, especially when Yarico was not there, so intensely did I feel my confinement that I longed to escape its darkness and the attentions of the creatures that shared my home with me. Relief came only with Yarico's visits, when she would stand outside and call softly, and I would appear and hold her close and whisper words of love into her ear.

My release from this confinement was abrupt and almost fatal. One day, a young boy of five had followed Yarico without her knowing. He stood outside the cave and began blowing darts at me and screaming from fear. I was very angry and dashed out after him.

'You jabbering ape!' I yelled, completely forgetting where I was. He ran off screaming and shouting, 'Caraibas! Caraibas!'

Before I knew it, the whole village was out after me, with all their deadly weapons in their hands. They carried arrows and bows, blowpipes and poisoned darts, stone axes, clubs, sticks and stones.

They caught me and, tying me up with lianas, dumped me in a hole with a bamboo cage over it. Shocked, I lost interest in the whole affair and simply gave myself up to my fate. My heart was plastered with hatred of Yarico's people. They were savages, and so was she. If they were not, why hadn't the young women prevented those crabbed old crones from throwing bones at me, from setting their scrawny dogs at my heels? The men were far more reasonable. With them it was a clean clubbing, a poisoning or a knife blade in the solar plexus.

All that night pigs prowled and grunted round my prison, and I woke in a spurt to the voices above me. Mostly men, they argued in a confused manner about something, probably my instant death.

Two stocky young men, their dark-black bodies smooth and shining with oil, removed the cage. One of them spat tobacco juice at me. The other man prodded me with a stick, all the while ordering me to climb out of the hole. The sides were steep and slippery and each time I failed to climb out the entire assemblage roared with laughter.

Even the young children ceased disporting themselves with a pig (which I later learned had been greased with melted fat for their entertainment), and joined in the laughter while looking down at me with their berry-round eyes. But, bolstered by my English pride, I managed to use my long legs to advantage and climbed out, to the further amusement of the crowd.

I stood a whole head above the men and so was able to obtain a full view of their collective faces. Those who stood in the front ranged in colour from dark black to reddish ochre and, apart from a cloth apron, the men were naked, their bodies free of hair. The hair on their heads, in spite of the boxlike shape of their skulls, was well-cared for. A few wore bamboo pegs through their noses and their eyes were ringed with black paint to enhance their ferocious appearance.

There were a number of Africans among them, one obviously powerful and feared by the assemblage. He alone wore a feathered headdress, a necklace of animals' teeth and a piece of puma hide over his shoulders.

The women, wearing hibiscus flowers in their hair, stood behind the men. Some had plaited their long, thick hair, but most had let it hang freely to show its dense blackness. Yarico was there too, like all the other women wearing, for the occasion, a fibre belt around her waist. I recognised her more from desperation than desire, although she was the single friend and familiar in that crowd.

The headman stepped forward and at that moment two men pushed me to my knees before him. The silence that followed was like a bird resting on each individual head. An old man, whom I guessed to be the priest rattled his gourd and scattered a potion from his coconut shell. Muttering an incantation, he broke into a feeble song and a lumbering dance, which his legs found difficult to sustain.

I smiled at the priest and he took this to mean a signal of my preparedness for some act he had in mind. He hurled some pebbles he carried in his pouch onto the ground in an act of divination, and then he drew a circle enclosing the pebbles, as if he needed more power to interpret the message. I glanced at Yarico who was seemingly in a trance. The oracle of the pebbles had spoken. Would I be a danger to the tribe? Men young and old rushed forward, some listening and nodding, others reticent and bewildered. The oracle had evidently not spoken clearly enough for the old man. He could see danger and, from the way he sniffed me, he could apparently smell it too.

He rushed towards me, peering into my eyes as though trying to find a pathway into my soul.

With a demented shriek, Yarico broke out of line and, snatching the flower from her hair and that from two or three of the other women, she rushed towards me and held the posy over my head crying, 'Lover! Lover!' in her tongue.

The assemblage buzzed like a hive of bees; such a flurrying proceeded as Yarico answered questions and fell to talking, with a fierce determination.

The chief pulled me to my feet and, because of his touch, I was purified and so made acceptable to the tribe. The old priest now pushed a young man into the ring and began a long harangue, on his behalf I suspected.

The chief turned to me and talked. I was amazed at the words I heard which, although heavily accented, were in the French tongue. All at once I blessed Mr Koenig with all my heart for I could understand the questions that were being put to me. He had seen, he said, 'Toobab or white men on the coast of Africa and they were brought by the sea.'

'Yes, it is true that the sea has brought me,' I replied, 'and Yarico found me. It is also true that I am strong like a pequi tree whatever that is.' If Yarico said so, I would admit to it. Yes, I was willing to pay Paiu, son of Paiuda, the shaman, whatever he wanted to save his honour as he was set to marry Yarico. Although I had little, I would pay. I had not told Yarico to cease from loving him.

'If Paiu would take my knife, here it is.' I handed it over.

'Paiu would take your —' he pointed at my breeches. I took them off and gave them to him.

The women crowded round me, amazed at the colour of my legs — a few painfully extracting their long blonde hairs.

'They say you are like a worm, a grub that lives in the belly of the world,' the headman smiled.

I shrugged.

Yarico and two older women began to rub my body with some vile purple paint. Suddenly, the flies that had been tormenting me stopped and went back to settling on the remnants of food sticking to the faces of the children.

After Paiu had accepted my breeches and my knife, Yarico was officially mine. I had no house to take her to so she took me to hers, and from that moment my life among her and her people began. A poem from my book came to mind.

'When we have loved, my love,
Panting and pale from love,
Then from your cheeks, my love,
Scent of the sweat I love.
And when our bodies love
Now to relax in love
After the stress of love,
Ever still more I love
Our mingled breath of love.'

I caught sight of Paiu fondling his knife and wearing his

breeches. To the fascination of a small group of boys he strutted like a peacock and then, on second thoughts, took off the breeches. He examined the insides of his legs and then yelled to his father that my witchcraft had made his legs sore. The Indians believed that all illness was caused by evil spirits which inhabited the world and could be sent to wreak mischief upon others. Paiu never wore his breeches again but hung them like a flag above the door of his house. I was, however, to see my shirt rot upon his roof long after I had given it to him.

CHAPTER TWO

Yarico's home and mine! A different place indeed from anything I had ever known! She led me through the compound
of Chief Tomo, who to my good fortune turned out to be her
father, to a house shaped like a windowless haystack with a
thickly thatched roof, and walls made of slatted palms interwoven with thick grass. An open space on one wall served as
a door to the cool, dark interior, a haven from the sticky heat
outside. Here and there hammocks could be seen and mats
made of coconut fronds lay piled up. Yarico's space was easily
identified by her possessions: aprons, shells and trinkets made
from seeds, beads and tortoiseshell, as well as gourds holding
flowers which she had gathered. Outside, roots and other
vegetables were carefully tended to supply the household with
provisions. Calabash trees had been planted to provide them
with receptacles. Surrounding all was a palisade to protect the
settlement from raiders. It was inwardly slanted so that when
the guards hung their hammocks behind it, they were protected from wind and rain.

   Chief Tomo, himself once an aggressive raider upon the
peaceful Arawaks on the leeward side of the island, had been
shipwrecked many years earlier. He had swum ashore with
others and been saved by the Caribs, whom he and his group
later dominated, intermarrying with their women and blending
their customs with those of his African homeland. They had
come to be called Black Caribs by white adventurers. The chief
was to give me a graphic account of the event much later on.

   I asked myself what I might contribute to such a civilisation, if Black Carib life could so be described. At the tender age of twenty, with nothing but privilege before me, I had needed no manual skills and had nothing to offer but sentiment well expressed. However, I reckoned I could teach these savages the beautiful cadences of my language and its songs and, with Yarico to help me, I would be certain to improve the nature of the Carib race to a prodigious extent.

Sad to say, I failed most abysmally, not on my own account, but because the Caribs were such a backward tribe of children, and profligate with time and ideas. Men, women and children thought my singing dreadful, not songs for polite diversion, but warlike chants for calling up spirits to haunt them for capturing me and killing my companions.

Paiuda, the priest, bade me cease my singing. So there I was, a useless man in the midst of savages who thought me a candidate for an institution for the lunatic — which was in their life a pit in the depths of the forest. The men sat in groups, plucking the hair from their bodies, picking their teeth, grooming the thick, oily thatch on their boxlike heads, and exchanging information that would be of no earthly use to civilised men. By God! Who would avow that the nature and pattern of clouds affected the fishing, or that the amount of dew upon the ground foretold the animals which could be speared at dawn? Who would swear that the colour of the petals in a certain flower affected its potency when used in the making of poisons? Who, indeed, would attest that the depth at which the blade of an axe was buried into a growing tree affected the efficiency of the clubs, paddles or canoes the tree was made into? The men discussed these things, their conviction as real as tears. They argued over the making of arrows, dyes and poisons, the rites of the dead and events in the spirit houses, and sometimes even fought over the rituals surrounding the clearing of new ground for planting each vegetable.

Sometimes the men would exclaim to me, while threading beads or carving gourds, 'Inkle, the forest is silent. It will rain. Can you not hear silence, Inkle?'

Of course I could not hear silence. It could not be heard!

Reluctantly, I would leave with them to find shelter and sure enough the rain would fall, and then after the shower, I would grudgingly concede a difference due to the silent affirmation of the gift of water by the forest animals.

To understand my surroundings, I knew I would have to give up my civilisation. My father had always said that civilisation could be lost and, remembering that, I decided that I would not give mine away. I stuck to myself, thinking my own thoughts and determinedly teaching Yarico to speak my language. She was an apt pupil and we were able to communicate in no time at all. I called her by name but never would she address me as Tommy because, she said, 'Spirits will call you away to their land of death.'

Her startling ignorance further established her in my mind as a child of the forest.

It was not easy to live in a community which venerated age above all things and hated all foreigners into the bargain. I was treated either as a child or as an idiot who could not be taught to hunt. I decided, therefore, to become a little skilled in the use of bow and arrow and told Yarico to cease feeding me calabashes of mess and permit me to shoot my own food as the children of four or five were expected to do. When hungry they either shot down plantain-leaf bundles of cooked yam and fish, prepared by their mothers and hung out of reach, or wandered off to kill and roast a bird, a mouse, a squirrel or a rabbit.

'Why do you act in this way?' asked Chief Tomo, when he observed my determination to shoot down my victuals like the children. 'Men must be men.'

'I am only a child in the knowledge of your tribe,' I replied. 'I will be a hunter in time, even though we are not hunters from birth in my land.'

'Bad luck will come,' protested the priest. 'You cannot walk backwards. It is bad!'

But I continued walking backwards and was soon able to hunt my own meals and finally went out with the men in search of bigger game. It was difficult struggling to 'see' in the forest, to recognise poisonous leaves and grubs, edible lizards, mushrooms, and roots and lianas that would stun and not poison fish, to appreciate the skilful interweaving of fronds and bark, and to construct a shelter and survive in the forest.

Until I had entered the forest, I had thought it a paradise of fruit trees, and teeming with animals ready to offer themselves to be killed for food. But animals had to be trapped and fruit obtained from beyond the dense canopy formed by the trees. To this area of the forest only the monkeys and other climbing animals had access and, in following them, men encountered the animals who preyed upon them.

All activities were surrounded by superstition and ritual, and many times I was scolded by Paiuda, the irascible priest, for violating some rule which they had absorbed into their spongelike natures from birth. Instead of always bidding Yarico come to me, like a high and mighty Carib man, I would approach her whether she was one foot or many feet away from the women's house. Paiuda's eyes would almost fall out of their sockets with consternation. By now his words of reprimand had become familiar to me.

'Inkle, you must not go so close to the women's house. You are a man!' Or on another occasion, 'You must not eat such ripe fruits. Your manhood will escape. See, you have no sons — not even daughters.'

'Ask Yarico why she prevents children from coming to us.'

'If the spirits call them, they come to this world. Yarico is but a woman. She has no power over children. They come or they go. Man is man, woman is woman!'

Sometimes he forbade me from hunting certain animals, and when I asked the chief to intervene he would say, 'Paiuda keeps the tribe and sings its song. You are not yet a man or a warrior. You must obey Paiuda.'

Obey Paiuda? Impossible! He was the devil on thin, bony legs and enjoyed the cruel rites which he performed when boys reached puberty. They were made to stop arrows shot at them, with a shield closely woven and then lined with boar's hide. If they failed, the arrows had to be extracted from their bodies without a murmur from them. Then they were made to run between rows of men, each flailing them with bamboo rods. This also had to be endured without a murmur. There were other secret ceremonies which were never told to me. All *that* passed me by for I could only win regard if and when I decided to become a warrior. Until then I was still merely a stranger from outside the community. In fact, I was an object that Yarico had found and as long as she valued me I was safe — safe from Paiuda, the shaman, and Paiu, his son and heir.

I went hunting for grubs with the children who thought my beard a joke, and that my hair (which had been bleached by the sun), was grass that the heat had killed. To preserve my book, which they thought edible, I had to keep it perpetually upon my person. Privacy as known to us was not given any consideration. Even at the dead of night there was always someone aware of one's actions or intentions.

I often felt like being alone with Yarico and telling her of my predicament; and sometimes we wandered along the forest path until we came to a waterfall which descended like a ruffled blanket of foam into the river below. One day as Yarico looked into the river reflecting the overhanging trees she said, 'We have to dance. Paiuda will decide if it is good. You will have to kill deer and catch much fish.'

'When will all this be?'

'When Paiuda says, "It is time".'

'What will you do, Yarico? You know I am nothing among your people.'

'As I would be among yours?'

How could I explain how different life among my people would be? She saw the world in tribal ways, but if we had to hunt and dance then so be it. If we did not, Chief Tomo would lose face.

Such times alone with Yarico were few and far between. Could we ever be assured we were alone, not followed by someone hiding behind a wall of leaves and looking at us? Paiuda could always design a snag or a trap for the unwary. We sat on the grass at the top of a hillock, the sunlight falling through the leaves and unlocking the colour of the waves beyond. From the hill I could see the wind worrying blossoms in the clearing below and I wished that some apparition would materialise and take me away. Failing that, perhaps a boat could appear on the horizon and transport me to the love in whom my heart delighted. For days I tunnelled through gloom asking myself, 'How can I leave this accursed place?'

Yarico had told me that her father had been given a Bible by a sailor and now used it as a charm; I was determined to borrow it and renew my faith in God by taking comfort from it. However, I could never easily find myself alone with Chief Tomo. It was as if the men, hating our talk in a strange tongue, conspired to keep us apart. They still excluded me from the hunting of large animals and so I decided to hunt alone. Rather than be forced to sit with the women and children as I awaited the men's return from hunting, I took to walking along the waterside where the sea deposited wreckage, in an attempt to locate objects from our ship. I found shattered cups and saucers, a rusty spoon and a flintlock that was in such disrepair it could not be fired.

The men looked over my treasures but that was all. No one coveted them enough to offer me any sort of privilege in return for them. I continued to scour the waterside, as they called it, and by chance found a broken sword. It was not much but it was, up to then, my most spectacular find. As I made my way home with it I saw a deer, exhausted from the effort of climbing out of a steep incline. The creature was in a pitiable state, waiting for its end. Every time it tried to get out, the sand slipped to confuse it more. So there it stood, worried by the flies, gasping from the heat and slowly dying. To cut it with a broken sword would have been to torture it more; I therefore made a noose of a thick liana and strangled it. I carried it back on my shoulders to find that, to my good fortune, the men's hunting that day had been poor. Four iguanas, a few mushrooms, a few grubs and a pregnant paca that could not be eaten except by children, were all that had been found.

I threw the deer at Paiuda's feet.

'Here it is,' I said. 'I have hunted well.' I confronted him, Carib-style, nose to nose.

He gave orders to skin and cook it and the whole community ate. I had fed them. They were all indebted to me. Yarico was proud of me. Not only was I a husband and a possession, I was a hunter and, with a bit of luck, would one day be a man.

I now spoke easily and often with Chief Tomo who, even though frequently in keen conversation with the men, seemed to be yearning for his homeland far across mysterious seas. I understood the chief's yearnings. Standing on the little hillock looking out over the distant sea always brought flecks of recollection that made my present position unbearable. I had been cast up on these shores like flotsam.

'How did you come to these parts?' I asked him out of genuine curiosity.

He gave a great blast of laughter and then said, 'I was sent by my king, the ruler, the King of Dahomey, Emperor of Popo, to this land. He had never seen a white man and then one day he saw one. "My God!" he shouted, covering his eyes. "This is a porpoise that lives in the sea." He asked that such an animal be brought to his court so that he could face it eye to eye. The people captured one in the territory close to Dahomey and brought it to the court.

'The king's wives shook with fear,' Chief Tomo told me. '"Aye, Aye," they whispered, "what is this thing? Is it a man? It eats like a man but it is not a man! Has it got what a man has?" The king took the man to his rooms where courtiers undressed him and made certain that he was a man. Everyone rejoiced and the king was happy that the man was not a devil. The white man became a favourite and told wonderful stories of the country from which he had come. One day the man began to pine for his country. He refused wives — even virgins — and cried for his gods.'

'"My friend", the king commanded him, "Go to your people and with you take Tomo, my trusted servant who speaks many languages. Take also three hundred and twenty pieces of purest gold and eighty of my finest slaves. Tomo will see your king and his wonders which can only be seen by the eyes of a wise man. Before you leave us, swear, white man, swear that you will return with Tomo. The slaves and the gold you will give to the king as a present from a greater king than he".'

'The white man promised many things and I left with a merry heart to enter the ship which sat upon the sea like a bird whose belly has been swollen by food. I entered joyfully, but once there, the white man put me among the slaves and treated me like a slave. He intended to sell us all to the British colony of Virginia, but first we had to go to Barbados with the cargo. On the way there we were attacked by pirates who vanquished our captors and released us on this island. We were without food and water and these people, who were themselves en-slaved by French pirates, took us in. We admired a way of life so close to our own. Many rituals were the same and we stayed among them. As time passed, we became one, and since that time we have put to death all men who come here, who threaten our way of life. You, Inkle, are the only one whose life we have not ended with our faithful clubs.'

'Those who say we eat men do not regard us as people, but as monkeys and dogs. We are good people, taking only what we need from the forest and listening to its voices.'

I was deeply startled by the chief's words and for a moment entered into the centre of his heart. I saw tears in his eyes and I knew that he carried a great need inside him — the need for his own country.

Yarico was delighted at my friendship with her father and promised to take me to visit her mother, whom I had thought dead, but who had in fact returned to her tribe because the women in this tribe would not work after Chief Tomo had captured her.

The Carib women worked all their waking hours. I could not recall a moment when the women sat around idly letting time go by. One day I observed Yarico from dawn to dusk and saw that she cooked the cassava cakes we ate, reaped yams, wove a hammock, scraped the pulp from the gourds which she cut, fished, waited on Chief Tomo and talked with great animation to people around. She still found time to swim, prepare the dyes to paint us and keep us free of insect pests, and look to her own beauty. It made me wonder if, being in such a primitive state of development, the women had little need for rest or recreation. Alice rested daily when she was tired after her ride in Hyde Park, but then, in comparing a native woman with one of refinement and good breeding, it was important to consider the delicacy of constitution.

I grew much closer to Yarico because, as she put it, the size of her love increased the more I became a son to her father. I never observed her show such feelings as anger or resentment to anyone on any occasion. Such feelings are a part of being human and her civilisation had not developed them. Men who landed on the island had to be killed. Women who brought ill-luck or caused the rains to fail had to be banished. For the whole tribe there was simply the rule of cause and effect. Simple rules kept Paiuda powerful. He indicated both the effects and the causes of things.

He disapproved of my long and intimate conversations with the chief and so one morning, his satanic eyes glowing like coals, he approached Yarico and said, as if uttering a threat, 'The dancing must be done. The time has come.'

Time! I hated time for its slow remorseless stealth.

A surge of resentment, nay of scorn, swept over me. Why should such an impoverished imbecile have dominion over me?

'I will not dance, except to the music of my own land.'

Chief Tomo understood not only what was said, but the manner of one as proud as he. 'Softly, my son! Paiuda keeps the tribe! He will dance. You will provide the feast.'

'Who will dance with Paiuda? The other men?'

'No. Yarico! It is the spirit dance of women!'

'And why is the old fool always telling me about it and why did he give the telling to the children?'

He shrugged. 'Because you must hunt the feast. Pigs, monkeys, crocodiles. They are not eaten at the feast of women.'

The old devil. I must capture large animals: deer, tapir or paca. It would be a difficult task since I had nothing to barter for help.

Yarico came to the rescue by promising to ask the women to arrange things well. The women compelled their husbands to help me prepare a deadfall along the routes where tapir spoor was discovered; and, sure enough, a large, lame tapir was caught a few days before the feast. Yarico and the women prepared the roots which stunned fish. So there was more than enough for everyone. As the food was gathered in, cooked and laid out on platters made of palm leaves, it took on more and more the resemblance of a feast.

I was consumed by curiosity to see the dance which was to procure me children by Yarico. I knew it was bound to fail since my love for her came not from the heart, nor from the soul, but from the cursedly devilish flesh.

Although no one had educated them, these primitive women used flowers and shells to beautify and enhance their appearance. They polished their bodies with oil so they gleamed and used coloured dyes to adorn the more beguiling parts of their person. Even Paiuda cut his fingernails, washed his calabash and cleaned up his face. The entire tribe had oiled their dense black hair as if it was a common head into which the wool of the African now and again imposed itself.

The day of the dance arrived and everyone journeyed to a clearing in the forest. At the appointed hour, the sound of rattles blended with the whistling of a bamboo flute. A murmur of anticipation ran through the gathering and Paiuda showed himself. He wore the mask of the Water Spirit and danced by jerking his head and thrusting his neck this way and that. As he jerked his head, he clicked and rattled his gourds until Yarico joined in, wailing and clicking in harmony. Adolescent girls, who had been in seclusion since puberty, joined in the din in order to enter the life of women. It was a weird, rhythmic blending of sounds and, while it lasted, the gestures accompanying the noise were compelling to watch.

Just as suddenly as it began, it ended and the gathering fell to eating. They reassured me that now Yarico had danced all would be well. The feasting continued until a ground fog rose and all hands disappeared into their houses to tell stories or drink cassiri.

How they could drink that substance was beyond me, for I could not bring myself to disregard the making of it! From time to time the women prepared cassava bread with manioc pulp from which the poisons had been extracted through pressure in a *tipiti*, an elongated tube made of palm-tree fibre. This flour was next shaped into cakes, dried in the sun and stored for eating with stews, fish and meat. If cassiri was desired, every member of the tribe joined in the making of it by merrily munching the cassava bread and spitting the residue into a communal container. This was then mixed with water and fermented. It is alcoholic enough to induce a drunken state. But I refused to put the drink to my lips because of its contaminated beginnings. However it was made, though, it loosened the tongue for the storytelling, itself usually a relaxing occasion. The stories always gave me great pleasure by having the quality of dreams about them — fresh dreams, newly washed, newly woven and true to the daily lives of the community.

Some of the nights I have always remembered were those when the moon hung in the sky like a golden fruit and the telling of stories began. After every ceremony, stories were told by husbands to wives, fathers to children and lovers to each other. Yarico's story, 'The Death of Ilele', gave me much pleasure. It was such a gentle convincing story that I remember it to this day.

'Ilele's wife, Sauwiki, was pregnant and craved paya-paya fruit. Every day she sent him to gather them until only those in the garden of those who walk the wind were ripe enough to be picked. These fruits were fiercely guarded, and when Ilele stole into the garden, the tree spirits captured him and took him to the sea. They changed him into a tuna fish and cast him upon the waters. 'Dance upon the waves,' they said, 'and shimmer in the sunlight and on the dancing waves. You are free forever and your wife and child will become like us, and be part of us.'

'Now, Inkle,' she had commanded at the end, 'Say our child will soon be born.'

I could not bring myself to say that. I had always imagined my son blue-eyed and golden-haired. I simply could not imagine some creature like those around me being my son. The blood of primitives can and does dominate. I was very angry with the Fate that had set me hither.

I found myself completely overtaken by feelings of sadness and despair. I dreamed that I was either under sods of earth or swimming in a sea of tears. It was at the time of year when the winds blew colder, turning men weak. I guessed that it was winter in my beloved England, and longed to race across fields heavily covered with snow, although the forest contained its own almanac of seasons. From reading the skies, Caribs knew when the rain would come or when forest fires would start. The rainy season was the time of danger from sudden floods, though when we were lucky enough to glimpse the skies through the sodden canopy of leaves, beautiful formations of herons, storks, flamingoes and cranes could be seen. Then Yarico would be a child again, laughing and twittering with glee. There was a gentleness about her at this time that could be found only in helpless animals or those that have been lost or maimed and then rescued, and I would look at her wondering what she truly thought of me, and how she imagined the world from which I had come. I'd ask myself:

Is she a parcel of ambrosia?
A swelling flood of loveliness?
Is she the beauteous lotus flower?
Is she a flowering tree of love?

And then I would stop and wonder if that was the right view to hold of a primitive maiden.

For the present, it was to my advantage to conceal the gulf of civilisation that existed between us. We understood nothing in the same way: friendship, love, kindness all meant different things to each of us. Her deepest loyalty was to the tribe, the chief, the shaman, the forest, the women and then perhaps the husband whom she had found cast up by the sea, two pieces of which floated around in his eyes. Her duty was to offer me protection from the malice of Paiuda and of his cadaverous-faced son, Paiu. She knew I had nowhere to go and no other woman could bear my hairy body, colourless legs and my eyes that were like bits of sky. There was no true love, although at times there was modesty, friendship, decorum of address and respect.

In order to spend time alone with Yarico, I had to say that my spirit needed her and demanded to be alone with hers. I was tired of the continual tribal scrutiny, of people never calling me by my name but sneaking up to me to talk, ask questions, or giggle at me.

I began to do things which amazed them. I wandered down to the beach and returned one day with several pieces of wood and succeeded with the aid of lianas to construct a chair and a table for Yarico to use. She didn't at first. Of course, she showed it to the women and, to Chief Tomo's delight, she put flowers upon it as he had seen done when he walked among the white men. Chief Tomo was an educated man. When I spoke to him about enlightened matters, I forgot his savagery and, had it not been for the colour of his skin, I would have admitted that the quality of his wisdom was not unlike my father's. I reflect, though, that never once did any of those elderly women, cleaning, smoking or drying fish, or carrying heavy loads that converted them into cart horses, remind me of my dear, kind mother. I imagined *her*, silent and suffering, working away at her embroidery, and praying for my soul. Poor mother! If only I could have written to her to enquire of her health and her well-being. She had perhaps grown tired of waiting for me to return. But who could remonstrate with her?

One morning, I caught a glimpse of Yarico standing beside one of the women. She seemed as if she hugged a papaya close to her body. Was she pregnant? She had never mentioned it. But maybe it was not the custom to tell the father about impending fatherhood. There was no one I could ask about the correct procedure. Both men and women would say, 'Don't ask about such matters! The Spirits are listening!'

The Spirits never rested. They worked tirelessly night and day, keeping an eye on us all through Paiuda and, in the future, through Paiu, the sorcerer's apprentice.

Next day I visited their hut and asked for Paiuda. 'Where is the old man? I am going to walk among Yarico's tribe, the Arawaks.'

Paiuda suddenly appeared.

'It is not the time.'

'How do you know?'

'A puma went to their village and took a child. It is not the time. The tiger must be killed.'

'Who will hunt it and kill it?'

'The men.'

'I will go too.'

'You cannot go. You are Caraibas.'

'We danced.'

'Your wife still has no child.'

'She is with child.'

'Then you may go.'

'Where is the puma, old man?'

'I have not yet seen it in my dreams.'

Paiuda sipped his orange and honey water and passed it to Paiu.

It was customary to offer the caller this communal drink after the host had drunk from it, for then the visitor could see that there was no poison it. But there was no friendship between us. Not yet anyway. And their mouths were full of yellow teeth.

I predicted to myself that the whole business of the hunt would be a long drawn-out affair. Paiuda would spend time in the spirit house. Paiu would play the flute to appease the spirit of the trees and there would have to be lengthy expiation for the shedding of the blood of a noble creature. I was right. The old fool rattled his gourds and began pleading at once to the spirit of the tiger.

'You must tell me your taboos
You must tell me what can injure you!
You must tell me what can strengthen you!
Without saying anything,
Let your secrets come into my heart!
You have a coat with a thousand hairs,
The arrow head will shoot them,
When Rabu has made that arrow,
He will bury it for many days.'

It was too amusing for a thinking man like myself. Yet there it all was. Already laid out. I had to survive as best I could. I was not of their society and all I had to do was to play their game. If Yarico was not with child, I could blame it on the winds, on the rain, the mosquito, her mother or even on a dream, though I knew Paiuda would say, 'What right have you to dream? You are not a shaman.'

'When will you have a child?' I asked her casually.

'When the rains come.'

'Will it be a man-child?'

'No a girl, which I will give to my mother, as is the custom.'

'Who told you it will be a girl?'

'Paiuda.'

So the old devil knew all along. Every step one took in that community was surrounded by silences, influences, secrecy and deception. Why couldn't Paiuda simply have admitted to being told? Why did he have to frighten me, undermine my confidence, cut the grass from under my feet, call me an outsider, make a fool of me? Why shouldn't I be told anything about the infant to come, even if, by tribal law, it belonged to Cocoro, Yarico's mother, whom I did not know? Ah well, I supposed the same things happened elsewhere, only perhaps no one ever heard of them. During her unannounced pregnancy, I actually looked upon Yarico as my wife and tried to give her care and consideration, but pregnancy meant nothing to her. She continued pounding away at the manioc roots, planting, grinding corn and doing all that she ever did. Her layette would consist of water, mosses and bark, all gifts from Nature. There'd be oils and dyes to protect the child's skin and she would learn to stun animals with her blowpipe and do all the simple things that a child of Nature would find it necessary to do. The civilisation contained in me would be lost in her and I would have to accept it and pretend it didn't matter. Would I ever get away from here, from these people whom I loved and spurned at the same time? And from this woman to whom I belonged for ever more, if I was not rescued?

There was little I could do to shift my thoughts away from myself and my situation and prepare for the hunt. I was just about to sit at Chief Tomo's feet to be told about its protocol when he too, like everyone else, hastened to Paiuda's house. I went too. Paiuda was sitting on his haunches, jerking and shaking in the grip of a trance, his eyelids locked like peapods.

'He is seeing! He is seeing!' they murmured. 'His dreams are growing flesh!'

When he had recovered he began to give individual advice about everything. He was the oracle and the gathering fell under his spell.

'Caraibas!' he snarled at me. 'Do not live in your head. Live in your hands and your heart. Your head is where the dreams are kept. When dreams grow flesh, trouble makes the bones.'

CHAPTER THREE

Everyone seemed to be bathing in the beauties of the sunrise when the day of the hunt dawned. The dew lost its own perfume in the scent of the earth, dripped in beads of silver from the foliage and gave a shine to the palm fronds, tossing and turning in the wind. Birds, long awake, flitted through the gown of mist left by the night; and Yarico, pleasure like a stain upon her face, her plump hips undulating, ran towards the river, patting those flower heads she passed on the way. She loved flowers and with a cluster held above my head had once bought my life and declared her love for me. I felt a sudden warmth towards her and followed her to the river.

She swam quietly, while I, a hesitant swimmer after my experience of shipwreck, struggled to keep up with her. Her ability to swim had always amazed me; her body so flexible and flirtatious in the water. She sighed contentedly at the beauty around her and, catching hold of each other, we swam out of the river and lay in the sunshine.

So great was my need of her, lying there with her hair outspread, that we did not notice the children as they crept towards us. Gesturing and laughing, they chortled, 'Turi-turi! Laugh with me!' Children learned early about life from the love stories freely told by the men.

'Go away, young monkeys!' I shouted, but they would not leave us, so curious were they about the world of adults. We swam out again and then returned, frustrated, to the settlement to eat what had been left there. There was no problem of who should eat. Anyone could eat the food, even the flies. Breakfast hardly ever varied except for the occasional clutch of eggs which we sometimes boiled and shelled. I felt content. It was futile to hope for more, for time to change its tempo, for rescue.

The preparation for the hunt was well under way. The puma's blood was to be shed. I wanted no part of it, but the forest, with its plaintive sounds and shadows, its voices and its mysteries, was to be found in even the youngest of the Caribs. The forest was a part of their being, like eyes and hair and toes. The men, dressed in masks representing the gods who would bless the hunt and preserve the hunters, gathered in the clearing to await the arrival of our shaman, Paiuda. It was a ceremony, this hunt of theirs, and every crumb of ritual had to be in place. The older menfolk, the lame and those too young to hunt squatted on the grass, the more uneasy among them cupping or strok-ing their private parts as was the custom of the tribe. There was no shame among them as white men knew it. They seemed only to exist at the level of the body, and yet they did not. They were stained and painted on the outside, but what went on inside them was much more enigmatic and profound. The tension rose as we waited for Paiuda to present himself in ceremonial dress. At last he appeared, suitably attired in gourds, beads, shells and a headdress of beautiful black and yellow feathers. Even those who had seen him many times since dawn stirred and murmured a little. He swung the heavy club above his head, visibly staggering with the effort. He then uttered a series of sepulchral cries and croaks, which later turned into a quaint little air:

'It is waiting for us,
It is waiting by the water.
We are coming, O creature!
We are coming with your death.'

A whir and rush of emerald parakeets passed overhead. Just as they disappeared from sight, Paiuda said solemnly, 'They are going. Let us go.'

Led by the elders, we trundled off, a rather untidy line, to the waterside where our canoes rested. Our water eventually took us to the sea, but because it was inland and fed by mountain streams, its water flowed fresh and sweet to taste. Even the canoes seemed to have captured the mood of the moment, and bobbed and swayed eagerly as the men greeted their souls. Paiuda, his head still resplendent, ordered the array of canoes, blessing and greeting each soul as it rose up before his inner eye.

My height very soon set me apart, and even when I bent double I seemed to paddle my canoe from the level of the head of our shaman's son, Paiu.

At last he said, 'Why are you a pequi tree?'

I kept silent but I knew what he meant. The pequi was a very tall tree with spherical fruits which boys at adolescence were encouraged to eat so that they could absorb its properties. I tried harder to keep my strokes in rhythm, but Paiu lost patience and pushed me aside.

'Stay behind there, Caraibas! Stay there,' he grunted.

I tagged on behind like a dog, a dog smouldering with hate. If by muttered curses I could have turned them all into worms and crushed them beneath my feet, I would have been gratified, so deeply had I been hurt! But out of my rage my father's words came once more to me: 'Think only of your advantage.'

There was nothing to be gained from throwing myself about in a nest of thorns.

I turned my attention to the scenery as I sat alongside the arrow-maker and his son, who stood erect in the canoe and shot at jumping fish. I faced the paddle for a very long time. I had never paddled before for such a sustained time and my arms began to ache from the hard usage. The arrow-maker frowned.

'You are lazy, Caraibas,' he said. He was a strange man who had clubbed his wife to death for touching the arrows he had prepared for bear hunting. He muttered curses over me as he heard me panting.

'Lazy dog, may you die of poison,' he hissed.

I had visited the man's hammock many times and recalled him smiling only when he had retrieved his arrows from the body of an animal of some considerable size. His son, Paku, fussed about him like a handmaiden, for it was his lot to drink down every jot of ritual surrounding the making of arrows of all kinds.

We paddled on towards the place where, by our shaman's divination, the puma was to be found. Yarico would have liked that place — many strangely shaped orchids grew there. The old man came alongside me in his canoe and eyed my legs. Compared to his, they seemed incredibly large. Was he suppressing a desire to feast upon me? 'Twas said that some Caribs ate men for the love of human flesh.

From the superficial swirling and rippling of the waters I assumed that the currents were very strong and by the way the flow resisted our paddles I was correct.

'Why are they going against the current?' I asked the arrow-maker, who by his gaze still contemplated my leg. He ignored my question, leaving me to discover that going against the flow slowed us down and allowed us time to scan the trees for our quarry. With the sun becoming fiercer by the minute, we kept up the rhythmic paddling, yet there was no sign of thirst or fatigue amongst these Caribs.

They talked among themselves and because I was forced to listen to their descriptions of the foliage, the scenery in general and the animals that showed themselves to us, I was struck by the exactness and precision of their speech. The tribe's survival depended upon the hunt. Its success was impossible without the ability to convey precise information and for this reason the men spoke to each other and relayed every difference or similarity, every feature of bush, tree or lianas, every variation of grass or shrub in the landscape with meticulous care. For the first time since entering the world of the Caribs, I could interpret the information and understand the literacy of nature. I looked where they indicated and then I saw what they saw and being able to understand made me feel happy. The expanse and power of the river into which our creek had vanished brought much less incomprehension to my thinking and as I passed through a forest architectural in design and symmetry, and layered in different hues of green, my dislike of my captors vanished. My spirit, that over time had tarnished like pewter, that morning gleamed like new silver, especially when fishes jumped high out of the water as if trying to peer through a hole in the wind.

The foliage cast varied silhouettes, some baffling in their intricacies, upon the river but the Caribs had turned their attention from that and seemed all at once to feel the same primeval tension.

'It is close,' whispered Paiu, son of Paiuda, and soon all eyes except mine had discovered it. After a moment of calm observation, I saw the creature arrogantly perched in the forked branch of a tree, its tail swinging nonchalantly into the gloom of greenery.

Paiu, son of Paiuda, was the keeper of the puma's spirit, for one had passed close to the women's house on the day of his birth, the ancestors in this way naming his mortal enemy. He began to tease it in a petulant voice:

'You are a fruit and this day
You will fall.
We bring your death. Show yourself!
Do not weep! Laugh! For we are laughing.
Death is the road to the ancestors.'

Paiu slipped into the river, swam to the shore and, crawling through the undergrowth, reached the tree on which the creature sat, its tail switching like a whip of thick liana. Paiu began to shake the tree, effort like a pie-crust on his brow. The creature did not move but the tree moved more. Now that it had gathered momentum, the Caribs added to the animal's unease by shouting in the most terrifying manner. The puma grew more uneasy and attempted to turn round on his perch. In the effort to do so it exposed a flank and then arrow and blowpipe leapt in. As the puma fell it turned and tumbled, and bumped into the protruding branches as if paying respect to all that had given it shelter. It finally dropped into the river with a resounding splash, the fragments of water like smashed glass leaping at the sun itself.

The puma was dead, and I regretted seeing such a noble creature so rapidly killed. We pulled it ashore and stood around marvelling at its beauty and its power. Paiu accepted praise with modesty, and watched closely as those whose task it was to do so skinned it. The carcass had to be buried and given its last meal, and one of the young men was despatched to kill it an animal. He returned without success and after explaining the problem was told that he had neither allowed for the rocking of the water nor the dancing of the wind before releasing his arrow. The young man tried again and this time returned with a fine young monkey which was placed beside the dead puma.

When we reached the settlement, carrying skin and head, there was much excitement among the women. The spirit of the puma could be honoured. After our own feast it was time for the telling of hunting tales, which had all been told many times before. Cassiri flowed and soon everyone was merry, the men openly laughing and the women smiling from behind their open palms.

The night brought a dreamy sliver of moon which made little impact on the darkness, but the hunters and other friendly relations gathered to celebrate the hunt all over again. More food and cassiri were passed around and then the men, with every crevice of stomach crammed, set off for the men's house to commune with the spirits. Of course, they did not allow me to accompany them. As far as they were concerned, I was not a man, and so with the women and children, I went to my mat and listened as they played the nose flute. Yarico, soothed by cassiri, slept.

I could not now tell who was first to waken but I can clearly recall my consternation when she asked me the question which all Carib women asked their men after a visit to the spirit house.

'Did the dream come to you?' she said, blinking to keep the cutting sunshine from her eyes. Blood rushed into my face for I knew she was trying to shame me.

'How could I dream?' I replied sharply. 'Am I not a child to your people?'

They smoked a herb which Paiuda carefully prepared and afterwards they drifted outside in a state reminiscent of the opium smokers of my father's club, 'The House of Lords', where he met the traders who shipped his cargo. Without another word she went among the women and returned anxious and perplexed.

'The men have dreamed,' she said. 'The spirit of the puma will bring others. We are no longer safe. We must go from this place.'

'When?'

'Paiuda will read the stones.'

Just at that moment, Chief Tomo, his stomach like an outsized gourd in front of him, shuffled in. It was unusual to see him out of his hammock at this time of day. But he was always welcome.

'My friend Inkle,' he began. 'You must be one with us. Walk our path, the path of the warrior, and be a son of the tribe. Let the stranger found among the sands die, and let a man of our tribe be born.'

'What will they do to me if and when I walk the path? Will they kill me?'

'They will see if you can kill yourself.'

I shrugged. But I knew in my heart of hearts that I wanted to belong to some place, some people, some world of hopes and dreams, however strange or nebulous.

The word spread through the tribe. I was to be initiated when Paiuda agreed to it. What did initiation mean? It meant that I could be polygamous, as was the custom, and have access to the mysteries of the tribe, and learn the meaning of ritual fruits and plants. I would then be led through the secret paths that reached the sea and the shore where I was first captured. No matter whom I asked, none would explain what was to be done to me. I feared scarification most of all.

The men avoided me, as a man from a powerful, colourless tribe, or so I thought; but when they saw my melancholy state, they assumed that since Yarico was so obviously pregnant, I was sharing that experience with her, as all Carib men do, feeling as she felt and suffering all her pains and mortifications. The women took great care of me, confining me to my hammock and feeding me potions and messes, and taking various liberties with my person. My every movement was supervised lest I infringe some ancient rite or displease one of the innumerable spirits that plagued their world.

Yarico had been taken to the women's house and in there, without any fuss, had given birth to our son, who would be handed over to her father Chief Tomo, my own father being unavailable. I could not bear to explain to the old chief that even if my papa had stood within inches of the murky creature, he would have had none of it. They named him Waiyo after the chief's African ancestor, leaving me amazed on two counts; first that I should have a child bearing such a name, and next that he should be dark-skinned and dark-haired, with a pud-ding-bowl of a face, naked of garments and stained with dye to keep the insects away from him. I had always imagined my son bearing the stamp of my forebears: blue-eyed and golden-haired and easily recognisable as being of Inkle breed and blood. Chief Tomo was the only person to notice any resem-blance, albeit of the fingers and the toes. 'Your blood shows clearly,' he said. 'It is everywhere but mostly in his ears and his feet.' Then, holding the child like a living doll, he danced to Paiuda's flute. Waiyo would grow up among the other chil-dren, cared for by all the women, while all the men hunted for his food. I paid him no more mind.

Among the Caribs, as among my people, children were simply adults in the making. The Caribs did not mind them much until the time of their initiation, when they became men and women. Before then they were the same as any other little creature of the forest.

Paiuda the shaman walked uninvited to my hammock and accused me of hindering his prophecies. Had he not predicted a girl for us, only to find a boy?

'You must be a man before the people,' he said.

'So? The people know that I'm a man. I am the father of Waiyo.'

'Yes, but you are a thing we found on the sand. It is time.'

What could I do but accept the invitation from the man who kept the tribe? It must have been something very difficult for him to do: to offer me the key to his kingdom.

The very next day, the preparations for my ordeal began. I became aware of men and women going in groups to the forest and returning with gourds full of something, which I could not decipher from their behaviour. They stored the gourds beside a pit the length of my height, which they had sneakily measured with a liana. The pit was slightly shallower than a grave, about four feet deep. The collecting of gourds continued all through the next day and the next. I inspected the untidy pile and was sure I saw something move. Did the gourds contain snakes? I sought consolation and reassurance from my wife, but she ignored me. Taking my courage in both hands I walked into the forest and carefully hid some rations as well as a hammock in case I needed to flee from my torturers. Satisfied with myself I returned and, with a troubled heart, squatted with the men who talked among themselves about everything except my ordeal, which was only hours away.

Yarico woke me early and after I had swum, she oiled my skin with a strong mixture of oils, and gave me a bark cloth with which to cover my back. When we returned from the river the sun was already high and the crowd, including some visitors from Yarico's tribe, had begun to gather. The women wore the usual hibiscus flowers in their hair, on the right side for the unmarried girls, the left for the married women and in the middle for the girls with a roving eye. The children, too, were freshly stained. I walked out, followed by Chief Tomo and his child Waiyo who was carried by a woman, Paiuda and some older men and a few adolescent boys who would lay me down in the pit.

'When Paiuda blows the conch once it will be time to start, and when he blows it twice it will be over,' said Chief Tomo. All I could see were Paiuda's gourds.

I was too preoccupied to take in more. He blew the conch rather feebly, I thought, for such a great occasion, and the boys sprang towards me and laid me down. Before I felt them, I smelled them. The pit was alive with red ants angry at being confined in gourds for so long. It was as if I had been plunged into a pool of fire. They fell upon me with a fury that made me either lash out or squirm until my arms and legs were pinioned. The ants now had me in their power and I could feel their mandibles cutting into me before they injected their poisons. Looking down upon myself I saw red beads of blood growing over my body and trickling down. It was as if my whole being was resting on red hot coals as the creatures tormented me with their jaws. The ants ran over me, trying to find a way out into the open and, in this way, entered every crevice of my body except my ears, which had been plugged with beeswax. I felt them in my nose and throat with every breath I took. Finally, I could feel them alive in my very innards, and sense the heat coming from their hard bodies, and their legs as sharp as pine needles. I could see my pain hovering above me in the light and my body pressing against my need to reclaim it. And then, with an almost maddening suddenness, I heard the conch coming in two faint blasts of sound, as though from a long distance. I was lifted out of the pit and laid on the grass. Everyone seemed happy. I had not cried out with the pain. Paiuda danced round me declaring me unclean and bidding no man help me. Then, throwing a club on the ground, he bade me go deep into the jungle and live with the spirits for six nights. Good men, he said, survived, because they were in the care of the spirits.

I did not hear the people leave but when I awoke it was almost dusk and I was alone. I could not help wondering what those vermin in the settlement were thinking of me and, ready to show them that an Englishman was no coward, I picked up the club with painful effort, sought out two pieces of flint and a bamboo pole, and set off.

I was in great pain. My limbs were swollen and I needed to reach the river. There was the hazard of snakes and alligators but I knew that by tapping the ground the vibrations would warn any predators away. When I reached the river, the water was still warm. I soaked myself and then sought and found one of the trysting caves that the women so frequently made. It was the most painfully uncomfortable night of my life. I could not sleep and I thought of the shelter I had so carefully and secretly prepared. But in which direction was it? Pain had obliterated all the memories that I had ever held in my brain, and had put in their place hallucinations that ran across the years. I saw myself once again a little child leaving my body and returning to it, as old and as wise as Chief Tomo.

By daylight, the itching from the ant bites had diminished and I felt strangely at peace. I began to recall the plants which the Caribs used for various ailments and set about finding them. By rubbing myself with the leaves of some I gained much relief from the swelling and the pain. I had once thought that the jungle was awash with food, but I knew now that finding food was no easy matter. As time passed I grew hungrier and set some traps which would produce some small animal that I could use either for roasting or eating raw. For two days I tried in vain to make a fire but on the third day, with a lot of skilled coaxing, the flints caused some moss to smoke and then to flame. I had, like a true Carib, made a fire and was beside myself with joy. I cooked the toads that I had trapped. They were fairly good eating.

My hands, though sore, were now no longer swollen so I set about building a proper shelter against the rain, if it should fall, but though the dew was heavy, the rain mercifully did not come. The rainfall was sometimes so heavy it caused a flash flood, and the Caribs knew from reading the weather when to take to high ground. That I had not learned.

However I tried, sleeping was difficult, and each morning

I would open up the scabs on my back. Beetles liked these little places on my body and found them even in the dark. While the beetles tried to lay their eggs in my wounds, I followed the eyes of the nocturnal creatures, or thought about how happily the Caribs would disport themselves if I died in my attempt to become a man. The implications for my 'tribe' would be severe. I resolved to return to them greatly increased in strength and without the least mention of my ordeal.

The following day, the fourth, I believed, I set about to explore the jungle more daringly than I had done before. I had not gone far when I heard voices. I had to conceal myself, for whoever it was could kill me. To the Caribs I was unclean, and to a raiding or unfriendly tribe my head would have made a good trophy. Two Iaruma women passed by and I was safe. But I knew now that I was well outside our territory. Had I been gone two days or three? I could not recall. How many sunsets had passed? Foolishly, I had lost count. In the settlement, time was measured by the rhythm of work, its nature and its organisation. There was no work in the forest, only the creatures which gave me inquisitive glances. Had they found my store of food? I was certain that Paiuda had somehow found and removed it all.

Oh hateful man! So crabbed and so full of guile. He must have sent the children after me as he did during the season of my assignations with Yarico. By silently reflecting on all that I had done, I realised that I had now come to my fifth day and thought how fine it would be if I returned home with a boar. Securing a sharp, pointed stick, I set out to find one of these beasts, fully knowing that if I failed at the first throw, I would be dead. I went down to the river and waited for the animals to come and passed the time by recounting all that I had done. I had made a fire, trapped frogs, made a shelter and searched for my store. Only two more days to go. I waited in vain. The boars did not come to the river that day. On my way back to my hide, I saw a trail of leaf cutters heading in the same direction. I took no chances and moved my hide.

I had begun to enjoy the solitude of the forest, the density and shapes of the foliage and the weirdness of thrown shadows. I realised how they had been the origins of beliefs in ghosts, spirits and the powers of the ancestors.

Something had changed in me. I had not become a Carib, but certainly the relationship with my surroundings had deepened. The forest had a voice of its own with its own breath and life and language, which could be understood by those who loved it.

That night, my life passed before me with a much more gentle clarity. I recalled my departure, my two brothers, the journey, the shipwreck and my Alice, who was with me. I imagined her lips on mine, her arms about me. Softly, cicadas started their song of love and I was alone again. With the blink of an eyelid, I awoke, a smile upon my face. Gone were all the feelings of being pushed into doing things by the Caribs. I felt well disposed to the whole of nature, but could not find words to praise it except to say joyfully, 'In wisdom, Lord, hast thou made all things.' Surrendering my will, I gave myself up to time and chance. To die among the Caribs would not, I was sure, be the worst death in the world.

I returned to the settlement on the morning of the seventh day. The orioles, which the Caribs trapped for their beautiful red and yellow feathers, were in full throat, and doves cooed from beneath the blankets of foliage and flowers. The grasses on the path seemed thicker, but with cautious and tentative steps I pressed on beyond the palms, the annattos, the yams and the bananas to the dwellings. My heart leapt at the sight of the living smoke which to me meant Life. Grunting, rummaging pigs blended with the friendly barking of the dogs and was like sweet music to my ears. The women, always first to awaken, had gone to the river to wash, but dear, suspicious Paiuda had expected me and was waiting for me with his flute to play me a welcome, as custom decreed.

'Old Grandfather,' I said. 'I have come back.'

He continued his weird tune, whatever its meaning, and then broke into a merry laugh showing all his battered old teeth and said, 'They found your bundle. Men do not do such things.' By men he meant Caribs. I shrugged and said jocularly, 'Inkle is Yawahoo.' (That is, I am a devil.)

His face darkened. To say that I was the devil was an apology, but to him it was a literal truth.

'Have you seen Yawahoo?' he asked anxiously.

'Yes,' I replied. With anxiety rising in his body to a visible flame, he pushed me towards the men's house and, by pouring foul-smelling substances over my head, cleansed me. Other men came and joined in my cleansing. Afterwards we squatted in a circle and when the correct number of men had come, Paiu, son of Paiuda, brought in a smoking pot and passed it round. Everyone inhaled and seemed fine, but when I took my turn I was overcome by feelings of the most unspeakable horror. I had truly descended into hell, where grotesque creatures danced and performed mysterious gestures before my eyes. The colours that encompassed the events were truly wonderful.

I woke to find myself on my mat with my mind still floating in a sea of shapes and colours, strange images and shining waterfalls. Large birds beckoned to me and snakes that became dancing women sat on my knees, but Yarico, wielding a spiked club, slew them all and turned me into a toucan so large, she had to tether me to a tree in the jungle. There was no dream, only these hallucinations which I could not describe to them in their language, so I used my imagination freely, creating the most impossible stories for them.

'The dream has come to him,' said the old man. 'It has come. All is well. What have you seen?'

I had seen nothing except the images, but why disappoint him?

'I saw you lying dead, old man,' I said, 'and then I made you well again.' He seemed pleased. He would never die. Yarico was as delighted as if she had won the catechism prize. She yelled to the other women, 'The dream is now with him in his head!'

Chief Tomo, Paiuda and his son now freely visited my hammock, each to tell me some important truth about the tribe. Chief Tomo talked of the 'Path of the Tall Trees', which he had found when he first came to the island.

Paiu told of another path that led to the 'House of the Sea Ghosts', and another to the 'Stream of Golden Water', which was kept by the fiercest tribe of all, who ate men when they came close. All these paths were now open to me, at my own risk. Sometimes the whole tribe went to the sea and the men chose their wives by chasing the young women to the water and taking those they caught and were ready to laugh in the tufty sand-grass.

Of all the curiosities open to me, I was keen to see the 'House of the Sea Ghosts'. First I had to let them know of my intention, through a story; and in the best tradition of the folkteller I told them the 'Priest's Tale' from Chaucer and, not caring what they thought of it, I inserted bits of the 'Good Samaritan' and the story of Jonah in the belly of the whale. The silence which followed showed that the sense of magic had won through. I again told my story and agreed with the men that we should move our settlement after they had tattooed me with the mark of the condor on my upper arm. It was a painful process, but my English blood sustained me and I did not cry out like a child who is hurt.

In the meantime, the women had been secretly preparing their large straw baskets for the journey, although a new settlement had not yet been found. The move occurred on the day Paiuda felt the urge to lead us on. Unexpectedly, he indicated the canoes which always seemed alive and ready. We paddled until the old man said, 'Here!' He pointed with his stick, disembarked, talked to his stones and motioned to us. No one doubted that it would be a good place, strategic enough to give us a view of our surroundings, sheltered enough to let us ward off attack and high enough to avoid flash floods. The women set to work to gather the thatch and all hands helped to build a shelter for the night.

The work of building the settlement continued all through the next day and then the men once more sat in their hammocks leaving the working of the land to the women. After several weeks of backbreaking toil the women began to grumble about the harsh toll the tough ground was taking of their energies. The men resumed their routine: arrow-making, brewing the poisons, setting traps and engaging in all the things Carib men did without concern for those who kept the wheels of their wishes turning. The women one day refused to work.

'We want others to help us,' they said. 'Get us women.'

'Where will more women be found?' I asked Yarico in consternation.

'From war. As my mother was taken. The men came and took us. I was not born then but I was made that same day.'

That night, in the men's house, it was agreed that Paku the arrow-maker's son should find any tribe and spy them out. He would hear the Iaruma for they wore little bells in their ears.

'If you are seen, they will take your head, but remember that your mother was of them and tell them she wronged me and I killed her, and now you have come to the land of her spirits,' Paku's father said. 'If they give you a mat, invite them to come and eat with us so that we can see how many they are before we make war.'

While Paku had gone, the warriors talked of nothing else but war, and when I asked about the raid, the men pointed into the forest and said we went there to the Arawaks, or there to the Iaruma or there to the Marau. It was always there, there, there! The women continued to withhold themselves and if a man tried to compel one, she raised such a commotion that the man and his family would die of shame.

So the war talk continued and became more tantalising each day. During and after the fighting, men took new wives, won regard and even prowled at night when everyone slept.

Paku returned without much joy. He had seen no Iaruma but had come upon some Arawaks. They looked few in number and it would be kind to make slaves of them. He had seen young ones among them and it would also be fun to have a strong woman to laugh with and prove strength also. The women brought cassiri and, after drinking all of it, Paku promised me a beautiful head as a trophy the next time he went to war.

That afternoon I talked with Chief Tomo and asked, 'Who is bigger in all that is good? The Carib who seizes people or the white man who also seizes people?'

'We raid for our daily food. We lay no whips upon our people. We don't brand them nor do we torture them. Death is noble when it comes in war. Your people took my pride away. They made a beast of me. Seal your lips, my Inkle, for one day your words will pierce your heart as arrows do.'

'Where will you raid this time and when will it be?'

'When Paiuda names the hour. We will not go to the land of the Arawak for we went to them the last time.'

A long silence followed and then he said the Arawak women were like beautiful birds, graceful and full of the sweetness of honey. But Iaruma women worked hard, were short and strong and were like flute music when they laughed. He had Waiyo perched upon his shoulders and walked back to his hammock as he stroked his huge drum belly.

I followed. A group was carefully preparing poisons under Paiuda's instruction. From time to time he stopped and shifted over to his pebbles, all laid out in the sun, out of the sight of the women. The poison now made, Paiuda began to dance in a set of grotesque steps. He then divined the auspicious time of the raid as midnight of the full moon. War was to be made upon the Warraus in two days. They lived on one of the smallest islands close to us. At the magic hour we paddled silently down the river, quietly landed and then crept through the narrow path to the settlement. The dogs that dared to bark at us were quickly silenced with our blowpipes and then, uttering our devilish cries, we invaded the camp. But alas, only the pleading of women and the sad whimperings of children reached our ears. White men had come, they said, and taken all their men to the place where the salt grew. 'You have come to save us, or else we must starve. We asked the condor to tell of our plight.' They could not offer us food and, instead of killing them, we showed them how to set strong traps and helped them to catch fish.

'We want women,' said one of our men. 'That is why we have come.'

'Yes, take us! Take us!' But they could not be taken. Women must be fought for and won with dried blood on the club and the head of the enemy for a trophy.

The men were both angry and disappointed and the talking continued far into the night, the shadows of the hammocks swinging rhythmically in the moonlight. They blamed Paiuda for having closed eyes and he, rather than suffer shame, blamed the length of time he had exposed his pebbles to the devil, who had passed by and harmed their power. The women would still not entertain their husbands' attention. There was disharmony everywhere: in the hammocks, on the mats and in the talking and the drinking. There had to be another, and this time successful, raid. The women oiled pebbles, one for each fighting man, and wished that enemy arrows would bounce away from our bodies, as we struggled with our attackers.

Each day the discontent in their hearts grew larger and sharper until, at last, the men picked on the Iaruma, a small, trusting, lively tribe that enjoyed telling stories and watching the wild ducks and other birds pass by. They also made beautiful clay pots, and hangings in vivid colours. There were only a few of them left, but they survived by keeping to themselves. From time to time they had traded with the Caribs, and sometimes passed close, for we heard their bells dangling from their ears. Paku had once met some and knew in what direction he should walk to find them. So off he went to invite them to attend a feast. It was the hot season. The hunting was not plentiful, and of course the Iaruma accepted the invitation. Once again an auspicious time was chosen and the feast duly prepared.

We heard the Iaruma coming and our women rushed down to the river to wait.

'Ask them to come and swim with you,' commanded Paiuda.

The Iaruma women accepted the call to swim, while we led the men to the cassiri, which a few of our older women served. The Iaruma warriors, laying down their bows and arrows, began to dance, for the cassiri had made them merry. Our old women saw their chance and slyly cut the strings of the Iaruma's bows and made them useless. A little boy, who had been watching unobserved, shouted a warning. But it was too late. The visitors had been tricked. Those who could escape did, but the majority were clubbed and the women and children taken. Those we did not want we sent away, and they went among those tribes that were related to them. The Iaruma wept at our trickery, and many remained intractable and would not eat. Paiuda continued to explain why we had tricked them.

'Are we not your betters? Do not other tribes fear us?'

But some of the women starved themselves to death while others cursed us and some of our people also died. Our women, though, were kind to the Iaruma women, watching them in the fields and deciding whom to choose as working partners and as friends. Yarico took two women, Lala and Zeze. Lala was about her age but wiser and tough, and able to shoot arrows and wrestle as well as any man. The men wrestled in a peculiar way, grasping the opponent's waist and pulling hard on the leg. The women from some tribes wrestled among themselves. Lala could fight any woman in our tribe.

Zeze, on the other hand, was sweet and fragile, fawnlike and shy. She spoke little, even to her own people, and was startled by everything about her. She had a perpetual look of surprise in her eyes. The war, the massacre, her life among us, had all left her irrevocably surprised. The more I saw her, the more I lusted after her. I wanted her deeply, for she would be to me a true wife and I would teach her about love as Yarico had taught me. I wanted to put into words my feelings for her, but could find none of my own. I turned once more to my now wretched book of poems, which had almost fallen to bits. I read:

She is lovely. She is tender
And her waist is sleek and slender.
She is sweet, modest her glances
And my heart she quite entrances.

If the truth be told, I was completely bewitched by this
young girl, whose youth lay so fresh and crisp upon her. I was
in the grip of an immense torture. I was being harried by it and
I could not help myself.

Does a Carib feel so sharply the pangs of love? A Black
Carib! I would have no qualms if I were one of them, deeply
one of them. At that moment I rejected myself, my body, my
heritage. The fear and feelings of condemnation were gone. I
felt only my frustration; gone were feelings of guilt. I would
have her, I reasoned. In my old world she was merely a child.
In their world, she was a woman. I would have her.

CHAPTER FOUR

Yarico suspected that Zeze was of more than a mild interest to me. Polygamy was part of their culture but I belonged to her and so prohibited from having any partner but her. She kept me continually in her sights while the women of the tribe helped with surveillance. Meanwhile Zeze continued to labour with resignation beside them. She took sly glances at me and looked away when our eyes met. Never once did she glance in the direction of the huts or the hammocks, as the bolder women did to entice the men.

The garden began to bloom; yams became more plentiful, ears of corn grew fuller and, with such bounty, peace and friendship returned. The rains fell and the rivers gave a bountiful harvest of fish for drying and storing against leaner times. Men, more relaxed, felt the sap of love rising and sneaked off to laugh in the bush with willing women. Yarico would not indulge her curiosity, although many men would have liked her to choose them. If she had gone with a man, I would have been able to reciprocate by choosing Zeze. Frustrated, I became angry at whatever Yarico did for me. One day I threw some fruit at her, proclaiming them rotten and, before she could recover, I tramped off into the bush, shouting for Zeze to follow me. She walked behind like a lamb to the slaughter. Reluctant and, I thought, unknowing, she walked behind me. She was no more than fourteen years of age with tiny fleshless knots of breasts peaking up from under her smooth brown skin. Her body, young and tender, had not yet been made bulbous with fat.

We walked on and, having found a suitable place, we began to build a shelter, she deftly weaving the palm fronds I passed to her. She said not a single word but her brown eyes widened every time I touched her, causing the release of the most profound desires in me.

I took her, gently relishing her virtue, savouring her virginity, making her mine and offering this innocent faun my soul. For me she was no heathen Carib, who stained her skin with annatto dye. I imagined her, even among the wildest awnings of nature, white-skinned and golden-haired and, like Alice, dressed in the finest and softest of silks. I held her close to me, a fragile and precious receptacle for the most rapturous moments of my life. Her lithe body made the act of love a rhapsody that carried me beyond the realms of pleasure to that time when a fusion of bodies became a fusion of souls.

When we returned, Yarico sat beside Paiuda's hammock in eager conversation with him.

'Ho,' I yelled. 'There is no need for him to read his feathers or his pebbles or consult his oracles. I laughed with Zeze. She is my wife. There are two of you now. I will tell Chief Tomo.'

They ignored me and continued talking. Zeze squatted with the other women and helped with the cooking. But that was not all. They closely questioned her, probably instructing her in the ways of women.

After the meal I talked with Chief Tomo and explained the situation.

'That is good,' he said. 'You are a man. But you should have told Yarico for she bought you blood for blood. Give Yarico a present and all will be well.'

Zeze was now fully my wife and I could protect her from those men who crept into the women's house to prowl. I had only become aware of 'prowling' after my initiation. It was the custom for men to creep out into the early dawn when sleep was soundest, noiselessly enter the women's hut, lift up their aprons, touch and fondle private parts and escape. If they were caught, they were exposed to the tribe and had to pay a present. The men made a great sport of this and talked of it among themselves — especially if the women never woke and they could amuse themselves to their hearts' content. On rare occasions, it was said the women paid them back in kind. However, many women feared and hated being titillated when sound asleep.

To me, Zeze was the fire of love rekindled. I was certain that I had met her before and I courted her as I would have done an English girl, walking, talking and kissing her all the way to the wedding bed in spite of Paiuda's remonstrances and cautions. Jealousy was unknown, it was said, to the primitive mind, but Yarico showed jealousy often and very clearly indeed.

It was Paku who, in a burst of friendship, now that we both had two wives, took me to the 'House of the Sea Ghosts', an ordinary but derelict house which had been erected as a kind of store house by a Frenchman whom the Caribs had tolerated until the Black Caribs joined them.

We reached the area by a circuitous route and then, after a steep descent, arrived at the seashore not far from the house. I could not restrain my curiosity and at once entered the house, marvelling at what was left of its interior.

Some of the heavy iron trunks it contained had rusted and could not be opened without sturdy tools but one or two of the locks yielded to my club. What some contained could not be ascertained, so thoroughly had the ants done their work, but in others I found women's clothes of various sizes and in different states of decay. I held a mutilated garment against Zeze to show her what white women wore. She shuddered while Yarico screamed, 'You will die. It is a spirit blanket. The sea ghost will kill you.'

Zeze began to cry for she was sure Yarico had cursed her with death, but knowing that Iaruma suspicions could easily be set to rest, I exorcised her by making the sign of the cross upon her head and saying a few French words over her. While she wept, I sang to Yarico so as to allay her jealousy and set her at ease. Oh women! They are like children who must be given the breast — even in tuneless song.

Zeze kept me sane. Her body was such perfection and her skin so reassuringly soft that even to touch her was to enter another world. We never spoke, but I could tell when she was pleased for she would approach me and sit astride my thighs and she would be mine. There were no obstacles of clothing and convention between us. We were in love and sex, constant pleasurable sex, was its natural culmination. She set me free of my captivity. She was completely mine, her womanliness so delicate, so magnificent in its expression.

With nature all about us our love attained a special clarity. Birds seemed to sing only for us; the breeze wafting over the river caressed us and, as we explored our desires, bade us continue to enjoy our union. Zeze, dear Zeze, never failed to take me far beyond the horizon, far above the trees to a place where there was only peace and the magical colours of the rainbow. It was our dream-time. A time of milk and honey in Eden, and I was willing to stay manacled to that life forever, surprised by both my love and my joy.

A change had come over me and everyone remarked upon it. Yarico no longer offended me simply by being alive on this earth. From time to time she visited Paiuda or sat with Chief Tomo and her son Waiyo, who had grown into a fussy, complaining child — not quite repulsive to look at but as unprepossessing as smudged stained glass, and yet a true Carib as far as I could discern. I was completely shorn of any tender feelings towards him or of any curiosity regarding his whereabouts. Chief Tomo, on the other hand, in affirmation of some link between us, always turned him towards me.

Zeze grew more into a woman, talking on equal terms with Yarico as they worked side by side, and afterwards I would steal away with one or the other of them. I thought constantly of Zeze and needed more and more to be one with her. My mind grew confused until I held her. Passion hovered just below the surface, always ready to erupt. Was I too demanding of her? She never objected. Was she afraid of me? What if I should lose her? I would hold her on my thighs, the tears streaming down my face as I felt her small wandering hand upon my back. Gone was all the consciousness of differences between us. She was a sweet and precious girl who, as we swayed and rocked, brought me delight in reality and fantasy.

And then suddenly Fate struck. One evening, I lay in my hammock marvelling at the stars scattered over the skies in myriad patterns. I drifted off. What my dreams were I could clearly recall but dared not! It was a most beauteous dream that went on like a play. In the heart of the plot and just prior to the denouement of the play I heard voices, eager muttering voices, interspersed with retching groans and shrieks. I recognised the voices as belonging to Paiuda, the wife of the canoe maker, two or three of the women who wove hammocks and Yarico.

'Inkle! Inkle!' she called. 'It is Zeze. The spirits want her! They will take her by sunrise!'

I jumped out of the hammock and followed the voices. Zeze lay on a mat, tossing and turning, obviously in great pain and moaning in her language. Paiuda squatted, rattling his gourds, certain that she would die as dawn appeared. He had made certain that she understood her fate. There was nothing to be done. Her ancestors, the spirits, and Paiuda had willed her death. Slowly they carried her to the women's house. There was a yellow glow in the sky beyond the trees. Dawn was breaking. I could hear poor Zeze's tremulous cry. I tried to call upon my God, but he had gone from me and the devil then sat beside me. All I could wish for was one last time to love my Zeze. Her groans reached me as if she assented and then there was only the silence and the tears, everywhere, the tears, my tears. How I wept for her! My darling! My naked brown bird, dressed in my imagination in the finery of love and wealth. Zeze was dead.

I was certain that Paiuda and Yarico knew about her death. But they could not have poisoned her for we had all eaten the same agouti stew. And then I recalled that poison could be rubbed into a calabash and remain undetected. I took Zeze's calabash and, filling it with water, set it by Chief Tomo's door.

His dogs were always thirsty and it would be a good test if one of his dogs should die. Treachery would be exposed.

My thoughts were on fire. I walked into the jungle gathering the flowers Zeze wore in her hair, and so felt closer to her. When I returned there was a crowd by Chief Tomo's door. Waiyo and his friend Toru had ventured out early. Waiyo, being thirsty, had drunk the water set down for the dog. Waiyo was now dying. It was pitiable to see his contorted body. I suddenly felt overwhelmed with feelings of hate, of pity, of love. I snatched him up, rocked him and rocked him, his squeals of pain fiercer now, his writhings weaker. Suddenly he was still. I blamed myself for putting the water down but the Caribs left food everywhere for anyone to eat and none had died of it. But my action proved how Zeze had been killed.

Chief Tomo began to wail, to sing of Waiyo. He told how I had been saved to become his father, how because I had become true Carib, Yarico had been blest and how he had inherited the boy by custom. The wailing went on all day. No one spoke of Zeze but my tears were for her. My heart, that because of her had soared like an eagle, lay bleeding through the lonely nights and days. I saw her moving in the dark waters of the river and in the glow of the moon and recalled the last time we squatted side by side without a word.

They buried her in the Carib manner as my wife, in bark cloth which they had softened and flattened. She was in a sitting attitude, her head resting on the palms of her hands, her elbows on her knees. Waiyo, too, was buried but as he was royalty he was buried under water. His bones would be excavated at the end of a year and distributed to his kin. Poor little Waiyo. Poor Zeze. Love was always the dancer at our feast and brought us joy and sweetened our desires. The warbling of the birds reminded me of her tinkling earrings. I could recapture her face but I failed to recapture her grace. When Waiyo lay quietly dead I could see his resemblance to my brother, Adam. I felt ashamed that I could not love him and sobbed a plea to my fate:

'Fate, give me any other ill you please,
I will bear it gladly. But I live among
Men who are philistines. Do not mark me!
Do not mark me! Do not mark me!'

Waiyo and Zeze, two little orchids, fell to the winds of Carib custom.

Sadness bound me to Chief Tomo. He lay in his hammock like a stricken man. I sat beside him, rocking to and fro to still the pain of grief. One day, he quietly told me that Zeze had been branded a witch. I had not known. It meant that anyone could have killed her. There was no mourning for her. She was Iaruma and the Iaruma women lived daily in a state of fear. More and more they escaped by slipping away into the bush, knowing that they could be attacked by animals or taken prisoner by their enemies if they failed to find their way back to the remnants of their own people. No one seemed to care what became of them. The ground had been cleared, the gardens bloomed. Zeze had been sacrificed. All would be well.

Yarico and I limped along. I began slowly once again to eat the messes she prepared, and we grew trust. We could see Chief Tomo's burden of grief more and more weighing him down, bringing him speedily to old age. When the children successfully 'hunted' packets of food, he glanced at Waiyo's bow and arrow, which had been left to comfort the old man, who now told a long-drawn-out story of the little boy so dearly loved.

Slowly, good times returned. At night, men played the flute and laughed with the women. During the day the sun shone, the storks stood motionless on a single leg in the swamps, clouds raced away to the ends of the earth and a solitary eagle wheeled and turned in the rest of the sky.

One morning, when Paiuda rose early and began singing stories, his song was cut in pieces when two Iaruma men called from the bushes, 'Hey, Grandfather! We will give you this axe. Come close, Grandfather!'

Paiuda approached them, although his family shouted at him to stay away.

'Come, Grandfather! Have you seen our wives? White men took us to the salt-island, but we crept away on our bellies like snakes and then swam like turtles, and here we are!'

Unheeding of death, Paiuda approached, rattling his gourds while chiding and scolding the Iaruma men. One of the Iaruma, seeing opportunity, immobilised the old man with an arrow aimed at his knees. But like a man of seven strengths, decrepit old Paiuda, made invincible by magic, walked on until the other Iaruma silenced him with a single blow to the head. After the old man had fallen, more Iaruma came out of the bushes, grabbing their women and dragging them away.

The Caribs, now helpless without a shaman, turned to Paiu who was unprepared for his task. He dithered until the Iaruma had made their escape. A whole day later we set off after them, but they had set traps and magic for us, and we found only two stragglers whom we killed. We returned home with their heads triumphantly perched on bamboo poles, but everyone knew in their hearts it had been a defeat.

The remaining Iaruma women walked round the heads with expressionless faces. They did not show any signs of recognition, nor were tears shed for them. They were with the ancestors in death, which like life is something that comes in its own time and in its own manner. They had died. That was all.

In time, Paiu proved to be an effective shaman. He knew the medicines and the curses and, having had a shorter period of contact with the spirits, he was less fussy and idiosyncratic than his father. He had a young wife and could not find the time to conspire with the women of the tribe as his father had done. What would Yarico do without the love potions the old shaman gave her? She talked of him as though he still lived and was a silent witness to all our encounters. Often close to tears, I thought daily of Zeze but the pain of my loss eventually disappeared and I once more turned to Yarico who, although warmly affectionate to me again, did not express any regret or sorrow at poor Zeze's terrible end.

Often we wandered off, Yarico and I, and sat among the palms, at peace with one another, and I proved that I was a man again. But often Zeze and Alice sat there too, side by side, causing me to feel a choking sensation. As I clutched my throat, trying to breathe, Yarico would weep for me in my sickness and ask her gods to protect me.

'Why do you weep?' I asked one day. 'Did you poison Zeze? Why do you weep? I had thought to take your life, for I was sure of your guilt and I am strong.'

She shook her head and replied, 'Perhaps Paiuda did. The stones showed that Zeze was a witch.'

'Are you sure? You must tell the true story.'

She nodded and continued. 'Paiuda killed her. She was a witch. She cooked and ate what was forbidden. Only Paiuda knows the poisons. She ate the poisons and lived.'

As I listened,, my hatred of Yarico melted, although I had not forgiven her. I could not do that for she had been a conspirator in the death of my gentle dove.

'Do you want more Iaruma women?' Yarico asked.

I shook my head. 'Zeze was young. These are old women.'

During the dry season, after the morning mist had lifted, Yarico, myself and a few others went out to gather honey in the forest. We were successful, for after a short walk we found a hive. We smoked out the bees and set off home with the honey. Yarico talked of having seen white men once.

'They came to our village and while the people fought them, my father buried their boat in the water. They started running and we caught them and killed them. My father took out their eyes. They were blue so we ate them.'

I was sickened by her story but many tribes ate parts of their enemies. I could have eaten any part of Zeze just to have her with me. We gathered shells and edible seaweed and then went home again. The sea always came as a surprise at the end of a long walk through the deep and secret jungle. If we were caught crossing strange territory, we would have been clubbed to death, but we took many chances and while Yarico swam,

I lay on the sand and thought of Zeze and recalled her lithesome body. At other times I sought to visit the hammock of Chief Tomo, who had turned suddenly old since Waiyo died. There was no one to open his eyes to the world of children. No one with whom to watch the faces of the earth. When he spoke his voice had begun to bury itself in the recesses of his body, and his steps were cursed with pain.

'When I am dead, Inkle,' he said, 'white men will come with their guns and they will kill or take my people to be their slaves.'

The island was divided into two — a windward side on which the hard wind blew, and a leeward side. The Caribs on the leeward side were able to fight off all their enemies successfully, for they were protected. According to Yarico, 'The men brought many heads with eyes like the sky and often the colour of toucan feathers.'

Paku also added his flavoursome bit: 'We took no prisoners because we did not know what to do with them. They chased us like paca and we trapped them like wild boar. Then we clubbed them to death and drank blood to give us strength.'

Chief Tomo also told stories, but they confused encounters with slave traders with those of shipwrecked or marooned compatriots. One day he clutched my hands and stared, as if confronted with a fearful memory, and mumbled, 'They came all dressed in skins of leopards, with great caps upon their heads, their faces painted white to make them fearful. They seized me and took me to the king.'

Another time he said, 'When we were on board, the soldiers brought me a liquid in a glass. I drank it. It was good! More and more they gave me. More and more I drank. Later my clothes were gone and I was chained to other men. White men betrayed me.'

As time passed, the lively spirit in Chief Tomo died and at night his sadness became a melancholy howling. Then one morning, after many weeks, he slowly, painfully managed to stand. Trembling at the knees, clutching a hard fist over his stick, while tears met the dribble from the corner of his mouth, he started on another day's long road. Shivering in the gentle breeze, he took the path to the woods without a backward glance. Yarico calmly explained, 'The spirits have come. It is his death day. He hears the voices of his ancestors.'

We all watched him go but no one mourned for him except to say, 'A man lives long who lives a hundred moons. Yet half is sleep and half old age. The darkness closes up the path.'

The next day a search party went out to find his bones. They found nothing for he had become an eagle and flown strongly and merrily back to his home in Africa.

The tribe began to disintegrate after Chief Tomo died. A new leader would emerge in the big hunt that was planned for the tribe. I was determined not to be a part of the hunt and conveniently dislocated my ankle. The hunt was to last many days, and those whom the Gods had sickened or made infirm remained at home to guard the women.

Yarico and I were now as close as we had been before, and we took to walking on the seashore, which we reached by way of the secret path through Arupati lands. I could see from her figure that I was to be a father for the second time. If only it had been Zeze, I thought. This time, I promised myself that I would do better! Yarico followed me faithfully for there was no more faithful creature than a Carib woman. She answered my every call, and even when I dawdled on the path that led through the territory of the cruel Arupati, she never reproved me and, although frightened, always followed.

It was good to be free from the squabbling Caribs for a while, to forget about spirits and taboos and to merely wonder who would emerge our leader. I could support neither Paku, his father the arrow-maker or any of the others. All lacked Chief Tomo's stature, though Maru, who fashioned the clubs, had a strength of character which was comparable.

There was a sense of freedom about the day when we left for the shore. After walking for hours we came to the beach, found a shady spot and sat engrossed in the movements of the creatures whose world was the sand. Facing us was a wall of trees with branches overhanging the river, but something was different this time. I stared unbelieving. I saw a canoe with two or three white men in it. I was so overcome, I forgot that they would regard me as Carib from the dye I wore and perhaps shoot at me. I leapt over Yarico who was sitting on the sand and hallooed to them. But the wind carried my voice in the opposite direction and then they were gone. I felt my disappointment like a lump in my throat. It was like a bewitchment come upon me. I was foiled by wind and distance.

The sand burned like fire under my body. But there I sat. 'Perhaps they will come back! They are my tribe! They must come back.'

Since I left my home I had seldom felt the need for prayer. Somehow I had to lift up my heart to my Creator and ask his aid. I lifted up my heart and I was sure from the intensity of my expression that it became a bird and nested in His Almighty heart.

We hung about the shore all day. At last, I gave up and bade Yarico gather her shells together, and we prepared to leave. As we busied ourselves we heard nothing, but some power made me turn and there it was, a sloop of war, like a painting at the centre of a diorama! A three-masted sloop! This time it was real. Its mast unfurled, challenging the wind. I hallooed like a lunatic and at last they lowered a boat. Two men clambered into it and began to row towards us. As they came closer, only one rowed and the other cocked his pistol. They were rough men who would brook no nonsense.

'Be ye Christian or heathen?' they yelled. 'Declare!'

'I am a Christian man. These long years kept prisoner by heathen Caribs. God save the King.'

They pulled me on board. Yarico swam behind the boat. If her strength had failed she would have drowned. Agitatedly, I looked towards her as she called, 'Inkle!'

'Who be the woman? Be she wife or slave? A pregnant slave?'

'She is my slave-wife. Can you not let her aboard?'

I helped Yarico aboard, where she sat curled up behind me,

in a state of exhaustion. I wanted to show her some affection, even pity, but dared not.

On board the sloop there were five other men beside the Captain, Master Dougal Fleece. He bade me tell him my story and I did again and again, for none could fail to marvel at it.

'Many men have been marooned upon these islands but none for as long as ye. The fever, the flux or the savages soon put an end to their miserable lives,' he said.

'I have had a good life. Often looking to my advantage.'

'I trust you desire to shave. Our boatswain is as full a size as you. He might perhaps lend you galligaskins. It ain't right for a white man to be scant of clothing.'

I was happy to be among civilised people again, even if they were rough. There were interesting men among them. One named John, who had been set adrift for being dubbed a 'Jonah', had been enslaved on some islands off Sierra Leone. He was kind and attentive to Yarico.

'What trading do you do?' I asked. He shrugged.

'I want to get to Barbados, John,' said I.

'I must go home to Ireland to be at the side of my sick father, but first I must go to Barbados to get a passage to Bristol and then another to Ireland.'

I nodded but did not really understand why he'd left Africa and must needs visit Barbados before going to Ireland. I no longer understood how the world worked, nor could I easily take comfort in the food and in the doings of other men. The rapid movement of the ship and the men upon it threw me constantly in a state of fear. How could I inform myself of my parents, or my brothers? I had spent nearly ninety moons in captivity. All the while my only thoughts were to escape from the Caribs. Now I had my freedom, and was made wretched by it. I had been rescued and I could no longer deal with my own language. English words passed over my ears as the Carib language had once done, causing me to forget who I was, and what I was trying to do or say.

Similarly, the clear light of day perplexed me. My eyes were used to the quieter tones of the forest, my ears to more natural sounds. Meanwhile Yarico slept on. The ship moved close to the banks hidden by the overhanging branches and from time to time, the sails furled, we slid into various coves to wait for the darkness which brought voices and mutterings and the clandestine sound of oars. What were these men doing?

I asked John again.

'Smugglers!' he said. 'They smuggle hogsheads of sugar, bags of salt, spices, anything. The owners of the plantations are in England, pretending to be gentry, living the good life, and the managers of the plantations deal with us, and Captain Fleece, our Master, fleeces them in name and nature. I knew this all along,' he continued, 'but it's naught to do wi' me.'

I smiled weakly, being offered so much to comprehend all at once.

'Tell me about her,' he asked, pointing to Yarico.

'She was the chief's daughter. She bought my life.'

'And you paid her back on the mat.'

'No, I married her. She's my wife.'

'That does not count. A marriage between a Christian and a heathen is nothing in the eyes of God.'

'She's very loyal.'

'Ha! I've seen some things. I was on slavers from the age of sixteen, and once out of Africa the sailors brought the women on deck and behaved worse than beasts.'

'Chief Tomo often talked of Africa. He was the leader of the tribe I lived among.'

'Oh, I've been among Africans for years. Some are rogues, but many value a good name and are honest, upright and trusting in business. The women are modest, until they are taught to earn more than their share by acting out the depravity that's in the minds of their keepers on the long voyage out.'

'What were you doing there?'

'All sorts really. I was a proctor once, staying at the fort to secure slaves. Then I took a job on an island outside Sierra Leone. The worst mistake I ever made.'

'Inkle!' Yarico called. Her face seemed strangely contorted.

'She's close to her time,' observed John. 'What shall be done? I've seen that look on the faces of native women before.'

Yarico pointed to the shore. 'She wants to be put on land,' I explained.

We lowered a boat and Yarico climbed in. She would not hear of company and quietly rowed herself to land.

'How does she feel to be so alone in her travail?' I thought. I need not have worried. Before sundown she returned with the child, a little boy — all strong and lusty. She had hardly shown her pregnancy. She looked much fuller in the middle but that was all. Everyone marvelled at the child, blond-haired, blue-eyed and very pale in colouring. He was my son all right. It was plainly there for all to see. I was completely shaken. I thought of Waiyo, so different in every dimension. Was he mine? No one will ever know.

The following day the captain visited the newborn child and the consternation on his face was something to behold, but then he recovered his equanimity.

'You sired the brat,' he sagely remarked. 'It would fetch a good price in Virginia. You will need money to get started and fate has provided it. You are a lucky man.'

I had never thought for a single instant of ridding myself of Yarico. Actually I had not thought what must be done with her at all. In some parts of my mind I was still back on the island, the No Man's land of the Caribs. Perhaps the captain was right. I must henceforward look to my advantage. The love of money is like a goad to all but very saintly men.

That night while Yarico, a blanket around her shoulders, suckled her infant, three women came aboard. They were part of the illicit trade, whatever it was, and made familiar and intimate sport with all hands on board, including Captain Fleece. The youngest, a comely black woman, native born of Grenada, who had fled her captors, marvelled at the child. The two others, white women with fiery natures, restless hands and raucous laughter which came like gunfire, praised Yarico's calm nature and beauty. She sat bewildered, amidst a civilisation, strange and perhaps ugly to her.

I offered her food, but she would not eat anything except fruit. Once more, John came to the rescue, offering her yam and sun-dried fish from his own store, for he had learnt to stomach such food on the shores of Africa.

Suddenly, voices became animated. The sloop had been detected by others, perhaps pirates. I could hear Captain Fleece giving orders. We raised anchor and put out to sea, the waves steady, the wind gently responding, filling our sails, and bearing us away to safety.

There is no more beautiful sight than moonlight on water, and Yarico, in true Carib fashion, began to croon dovelike to her child. Something stirred in me and my heart once more turned to my brothers and to Alice. I sat close to Yarico. From time to time she turned and looked at me — shaven, groomed and wearing clothes and native straw slippers. I believe she did not recognise me as the man of the island.

John joined us.

'Was it like this with you?' I said. 'Native wife and child?'

'Oh, no. I did indulge my feelings, to my shame. But now God has visited me and I am altered. I have been cleansed, freed from lust.'

'Where were you in Africa?'

'Oh, it's a long story and it sickens me to tell it, but tell it I will. I met up with an Englishman, a slave trader who invited me to live with him on an island off the coast of Sierra Leone. The island was a low sandy place covered with pale trees and we decided to build a house and grow limes there. I got on well with him until he fell in love with a domineering black woman who led him round like a dog on a lead. She was person of consequence and through her he filled his ships with slaves. I had no feelings either of love or hate against her, but she saw me as intruding into a blissful relationship and set out to torment me and show that she did not care much for white men. She loathed me from the start and set out deliberately to taunt and persecute me when the master was absent. After I'd been on the island some little time, I contracted a fever, but the woman, whom I would not describe as comely, gave me a wooden chest for a bed and a log for a pillow.'

'Did you never bring her behaviour to the attention of your master?' I interposed.

'Of course. But he never believed me. So great was his love for her. Behind his back she ordered her slaves to taunt and stone me and deny me food and water, so that I dug for roots to sustain my life. He would heed no complaint against the woman, even from a man of his own race. She was Jezebel incarnate! A harridan! A witch, who kept the man bewitched!'

'You are away from all that now and must be well content?'

'Oh yes. One day, I will return there and face them both as a man of honour. She was truly evil. One day, although she had seen me weak with fever, she threw victuals on the ground commanding me to pick them up. I remember that well.'

'They are no better in Newgate,' Billy the mate chimed in. 'Twice I was held there for highway robbery. Me and my Bessie. She for relieving a rich old woman of handkerchiefs and a bolt of linen, and me for demanding ten sovereigns from a wool merchant. They found me in an outhouse, where but for a barking dog I would have been safe.'

'I thought the mob hanged prisoners at once.'

'Don't be such a dupe, Inkle. Things are done proper in England. There is a judge and you goes before him and he passes either death or transportation upon you.'

'How did you slip the noose, Billy?'

'Aye, my Bessie! She whispered sweet nothings into the keeper's ear. She worms her way into his confidence and succeeds in selling him his own gold watch and borrowing his keys to release me. Poor man! So keen to tread a measure with my Bess.'

'Where is Bessie now?'

'Bessie!' he hollered and one of the two white women, as foul-mouthed as ever, appeared. I then realised I was in a nest of vipers of both sexes.

A voice was heard, a voice rising and falling in cadences. The men looked at each other and burst out laughing. Noticing my bewilderment they explained, 'When Captain Fleece, a learned man, is drunk, he recites lines from what he calls the *Dunciad*, poems writ by gentry.' The captain, John added, was the black sheep of his family and thus had been abandoned to the colonies as a rake and a dissolute.

Yarico's child began to cry and she asked for water. I fetched her some, taunted and teased by all save John, who said they should not mock a heathen, and chided them for not knowing their Christian duties.

Next morning, the captain told us that we would have to lie up among the coves until the pirates hunting us had departed in search of more worthy prey. Although we had between ten to thirty small calibre guns on one deck, the pirate ships carried much larger guns. To challenge them was to be annihilated.

All our crew had by now returned and I discovered that there were many more than I had at first counted. Yarico still sat in her corner, feeling the oppression of close contact with people she did not know, and whom she feared would destroy her. But the men ignored her for they knew that Captain Fleece kept his crew in good shape and sound control. 'When he flogs, he sets no limit to the punishment,' they said wryly.

With the ageing of the day, Yarico now seemed brighter. She had asked to be put ashore several times. What she did there no one knew but I suspected that she tried to communicate by some means with her mother's tribe, which we had never managed to visit, although we had talked of it. From time to time I looked at the baby and he seemed fine. I was even getting to like the little chap. I didn't name him for whatever name he had would be changed when he was sold, and this I had resolved to do. I needed decent clothes, an inn to stay and sundries with which to survive to make myself presentable to society. I explained very carefully to Yarico that things were different between us, that the child might be sold but would live on in memory. She smiled and nodded. She was evidently happy for him to be sold.

'When?' she suddenly asked.

'When we come to Barbados,' I replied. 'I will make sure he

falls into good hands. I will not have him flogged. You are beautiful, Yarico. Another is bound to love you. I will have to leave you and return to my people.'

She rolled her eyes and then smiled as though she saw something strange in the distance. And again she said nothing.

We continued sailing close to the shore, going round and round little islands and hiding in the bays and coves. In the evenings we moored and lay listening for those who sought to discover us. The rest of the company left us alone, and the captain stayed silent and sober in his berth with his lover, his beautiful black slave, to comfort him. I asked John where she had been captured.

'She is not a slave. He hired her from a brothel run by a trader in Grenada and never returned her.'

'Will she always remain on this sloop-of-war?'

'Until he tires of her. Then she'll be put ashore to fend for herself.'

Was this the world I longed to return to? At that moment I resolved to protect Yarico. I would not plot against her person. She was not a slave, therefore I would not expose her to slavery nor sell my son. At that moment I resolved also to build a house such as we had on the island and live there in peace and amity, with my wife and my son who, at that moment, I decided to name Adam after my brother.

That night, as I lay on deck wondering to what world the sea would finally take me, I recalled my life among the Caribs. Who was I to call them savage or primitive or fierce? Our people were no better. They believed in a Christian God and used this as a justification of depriving the slaves of belief, language and the kind of customs by which Paiuda kept his people together. The wind rose over the sea making surf against the bows. The child whimpered. The men, now out in the open sea, sang shanties. We were heading for Barbados.

It was a strange feeling. I should have visited that island seven years ago on business for my father. Panic seized me. Time hung in the air like a buzzing bee. Perhaps my father was dead. My mother too. And my brothers, what of them? My first task would be to find a shelter for my family and then continue the business with our family estates I had begun years earlier. My heart was heavy and filled with love of Alice, but she had to be placed alongside my duty to my family. I felt better after clear thought and ate a hearty breakfast and pondered my resolutions.

When John came on deck, I once more questioned him about the speed with which I might obtain accommodation for my family upon reaching Barbados. His eyes widened; his nose twitched; he scratched his face.

'A man of your quality,' he stuttered. 'Oh no, you won't be able to keep her around you, oh no!'

'Why?'

'In another island she might be kept as a mistress, but "wife" is only kept for ladies from Europe and being a Carib, well, her work will be outside, in the fields. If you want a mistress, there'll be plenty of mustees and mulattoes willing to oblige. I bid you make no plans but hasten to be rid of her.'

John's words set my heart spinning. I could do nothing but await my arrival upon the island.

CHAPTER FIVE

Bridgetown was crowded with shipping: large barques, brigs, cutters, merchantmen and frigates. We pulled alongside a schooner and all the sailors scuttled off on shore. Only the captain and Awana remained on board with Yarico and the child.

'I have instructed the boatswain to show you to the tailor,' said Captain Fleece. 'He will make you a suit of clothes and everything else you need. In cut and bearing you are what I once was — a gentleman.'

'But I will…'

'Gentlemen never mention money. Your needs are all that matter,' said Captain Fleece.

I bade Yarico goodbye and went on land.

It was a beautiful place with shady trees and wharf-houses. The land was pleasantly undulating, the prevailing colour a clear, clean green from the surrounding sugarcane fields. The people moved around industriously. At last we reached the principal street. The shops of the jewellers shone brightly in the sunshine and the merchandise on display reflected its genesis in all parts of the globe. I saw no sullenness among the slaves loading and unloading the ships. They worked with great concentration. Those who were too old to work begged from the gutters, for I was soon to discover that little provision was made for those too old to work.

The tailor, an obsequious Irishman, told me that my clothes would be ready in a day or two. After I had chosen the material I had fully intended to return to Yarico, but the captain would not hear of it. Instead, he took me to the plantation of a wealthy planter who said to me, 'My house is your house, Mr Inkle. I have been told of your adventure. I can assure you it is most remarkable and our people in England shall hear of it. Meanwhile, Claudia will bring you all you need.'

I shaved again and Claudia, a mulatto maid, brought me a crisp, short-sleeved, white collarless shirt and cotton trousers, slightly slack in the waist and floppy in the legs.

'Tea be at four o'clock, Massa Inkle,' she said.

I listened for the bell and answered by going into the dining room. The sight of an English tea-table filled my heart with joy. I could hardly contain myself, and wept. There were no women to remonstrate with me and Claudia, as a slave, did not interfere.

The planter, Mr Tim Dunbar, Claudia explained, had inherited the plantation from his sister, and he lived there cared for by devoted staff.

'Never worry about a t'ing, Massa Inkle,' she said. 'Settle down. Nice to be wid you own people again. Massa Dunbar does come and does go. He own plantation in Georgia also.'

I did not enjoy my tea. The texture of the meat and cakes, the smell of the food, the effect on my palate were all totally nauseating. I missed the Carib food and lay thinking of the past until the sun started to sink. The field slaves were coming home, each with a bunch of plantains for their Sunday fare. I had not even realised that it was Saturday. I watched them entering their huts, their lights flickering in the darkness. The stars twinkled overhead and when it was dark enough the creatures of the night made music and the fireflies danced to it.

Claudia brought me a toddy and asked again, 'You want anyt'ing, Massa-Sah? You need any odder thing to celebrate you homecoming?' I assured her I did not.

The feel of the bed underneath me was uncomfortable. Did one need such an enormous contraption? A hammock was both economical and convenient. I needed to sleep but not in a bed. I lay on the floor and fell fast asleep.

I was awakened by Claudia's screams.

'Lord-a-mercy,' she screamed. 'Lord-a-mercy. Massa Inkle done dead here on de floor. Sancho, come quick. Massa Inkle done dead!'

I sat up. 'I am not dead, Claudia. I could not sleep in a bed after years of sleeping on a mat or in a hammock.'

'Massa Inkle, you de first white man who never like a bed. A bed is natural to a massa as a shirt is natural to a massa. You's tea's getting cold!'

She dropped the cup on the table, spilling its contents, and then disappeared.

Later, Tim Dunbar visited me in my room. 'Claudia is not very respectful, but her heart is in the right place. You go down to the slave market and buy a parcel of slaves, but you never know how much hatred, resentment and cunning you've bought. One has to be careful not to offend them. They are knowledgeable about poisons.'

'The Caribs were the same.'

'Yes, Caribs,' he replied contemplatively. 'Special rules are applied with regard to them. I understand you have one.'

'Yes. I'll take you to her.'

'I want to buy her. I hear she is of a good breeding age. We have to be careful not to be seen ill-treating them publicly. There are secret abolitionists here. People who resent slavery.'

The reason for this was obscure to me yet I asked no questions. This man dealt daily in such matters. Who was I to question him?

I made myself as much satisfied with all about me as I could, although the forest with its voices and its powers welled up in me from time to time. I recalled the unsophisticated ways of the Carib men, their lack of guile and subterfuge, the free laughter of the children and the unpretentiousness of the women. They were unfettered in heart and limb, fearing only the ghosts and demons they had never seen.

The slaves puzzled me. I could read every inch of the Caribs. I knew from long association with them what they thought; but the slaves smiled and talked so only their brethren could understand them. They obeyed white people in such a way that it became a mockery. The women seemed subdued, yet they smouldered and listened like lizards. It was, I feared, going to be a hard and deep river for me to cross, with or without Yarico.

Early the next day, and full of trepidation, I set out to visit her. I was unsure what it was that I felt for her. Was it pity, compassion, sympathy or love? I wished I could discuss her plight with John, who had been so kind to her, but he was determined to get a passage home however he could.

My life among the Black Caribs continued to haunt me and I realised that I had put down invisible roots among them, and had been nourished by the life. There was a wisdom and a harmony about them that no longer existed in my present condition. I recalled the watching, the listening, the trapped animals, the trees dripping with dew, the pebbles, the marvellous forms of Nature. There I was expected to know nothing for I was no longer of the master race. Here in Barbados I was expected to know all things. Was I not a superior white man and so, omnipotent and infallible? In fact, I was lost within myself. I took comfort though in the belief that had not God marked me for survival, I would have been like my shipmates: bones whitening in the sun. Quelling anxieties, I walked in the sumptuous grounds, overladen with flowering trees, and palms of the most intricate species. I began to think for the first time for years of the original purpose of my journey to the West Indies. There was the family estate to inspect. I laid more of my past before Dunbar and he arranged for letters to go to England to provide me proof of identity and fresh instructions from my family. In the meantime, Dunbar, the soul of kindness, urged me to stay on his estate where I might learn something of sugar and its cultivation. He sought intelligence of our estate and was able to inform me that it was honestly and effectively managed. All would be well, I thought. All would surely be well.

Yarico, who was still billeted on the sloop, was greatly altered since I had last seen her. Her hair now fell in a soft, dark shower upon her shoulders, giving her face a longer sweep of expressions than was normal for her. She wore a length of red material wrapped round her waist and carried her baby in a hammock across her back in a matching piece of cotton secured in front by a large knot. She looked fresh and pleasing to the eye and animatedly said that Avana and Stella, two of the women on the three-masted sloop-of-war, had brought some Caribs to talk with her.

'Where are they now?' said I. 'Those helpful women?' She shrugged, dancing her shoulders Carib fashion, her gaze lost in the distance. There seemed to be a fire ablaze inside her head.

Dunbar and I exchanged glances to show that we had agreed.

The transaction was to be immediate. He thereupon proceeded to examine her in every detail. Having satisfied himself that she was physically in fine condition, he suddenly thrust the hundred and thirty pounds into my hands. I accepted the money knowing at that moment how all betrayers of trust must feel. Only the deceitful kiss was missing, and that I could not give her in the presence of another white man!

I stood close to her and said, 'You are sold, Yarico. To this gentleman, Mr Dunbar. He will take you to your island and there set you down and your people will find you as you found me.'

Her head tilted, she peered accusingly at me and then rasped, as only a Carib can, 'If he carry me to my people, why he give *you* present? Why you not give *him* present?'

'She's no fool,' Tim observed. Then turning to her he said, with menace in his voice, 'I am your master. Be sure you obey me. See those slaves waiting to be taken on board ship?'

She raised her eyes but looked towards the sea as if formulating some devilish plan. Dunbar pushed her firmly in the direction of the slaves awaiting their fate. They were manacled and she heard the clanking of their chains. With true Carib intuition she knew the truth before Dunbar's slave chained her, and for a moment she held my gaze as if challenging me to toy with her soul. To calm myself I once more reassured Dunbar that I was indeed the father of the child then, turning again to her, I remarked, 'They are going home, Yarico. Today. On the boat, the big boat, when the tide turns. Stand with them for you would be taken to your island also.'

The mention of the tide must have caused something to coalesce in her mind, for she rushed to the full extent of the chain and wrenching the child from her breast she whirled him above her head like a bull-roarer. He shrieked like the spirit of the bull-roarer, as she tossed him with a piercing scream into the sea. I watched the surf close over him and knew he was no more. She stared at the waves rolling over as if looking into a mirror of horrors, and then she smiled even as the slave driver unceasingly lashed her for her act of defiance. She showed no emotion whatsoever. It was as if he had stroked her with a bunch of feathers. Then out of the very centre of her being she turned to me and groaned.

'They will come! They will come! Like the moonlight shadows they will come.' She snapped the stick she had picked up to hit me with and threw it into the sea. The suddenness of her action surprised me. But it should not have done so for the Black Caribs did not view children as people until they were a year old. They were simply little creatures, like monkeys or fishes or birds. The women suckled little animals at the same time as they suckled their children. In Yarico's heart was spite alone. No one would own her pet monkey — albeit a beautiful one. As these thoughts whirled about in my head a sailor touched me on the shoulder. He had netted the child for his own sport. The child looked like a creature from a petrified forest. Every trace of the resemblance to my brother Adam had vanished from his face. Yarico gave a little cry, almost like that of one of those animals we used to trap in the morning time of our love. I wanted to comfort her and tell her once again what I knew to be a lie. Instead I said, 'This is too terrible, Dunbar. No more of it.'

He led me away and replied, 'Sometimes in this trade one has to eat off a very dirty plate, my friend. There is small space for pity,' and led me from the quay side.

The roads were crowded with planters, slaves and servants, but they did not interest me. I just could not help thinking about what was regarded as civilisation. I had no real love for the Black Caribs, but out there in the jungle Yarico and I had found a path that we could follow, while here on an island of what was regarded as civilised people, life for us had become divided by an abyss so deep that it had turned to corruption and deceit. Yarico's face kept haunting me and I shivered with remorse in the hot afternoon air. Dunbar, however, was in a gay mood and slipped into a side street which led us to the door of his club, a uniformed slave in attendance. He, big, burly and shining, showed us to a panelled room which closely resembled the one in which my father had sat with his friends making bargains and hatching plots to empty other traders' purses. It was as if that room had been dismantled and brought to this land, lock, stock and barrel. Several men dressed in tropical clothes wore the same expression as my father and his friends. They pored over a large map, deftly moving little cardboard ships over the seas and the oceans. They seemed a breed of men found wherever others bought, sold or bartered goods or traded in men, women and children as though they were the beasts of the earth. The gathering was in high spirits as trade was then good and so the talk turned to bargaining, arguing and then to querulous drinking. They were all kith and kin, white and English with the power of life and death over those they owned and branded as their own. Despite the fact that my family owned an estate, I felt left out of these discussions about property. In many ways my experience of the civilised world had stopped when I was twenty. I again refused a drink. All eyes were now turned towards me, some faces quizzical, the lips of others curled with incomprehension. Seeing that I would soon come in for unfavourable scrutiny, Dunbar jokingly said, 'He is suffering from an overdose of conscience. He has sold his Carib, and the silly creature saw fit to drown the offspring made by this fine specimen of a man.'

Hoots and guffaws could be heard echoing through the rooms, and I suppose I must have blushed for the merriment broke out afresh. I tried to speak but could find nothing to say. Yet the men still laughed as though enjoying a ribald play.

'Oh,' said Dunbar suddenly. 'I'm forgetting my manners. Gentlemen,' he bowed with exaggerated courtesy, 'this is Thomas Inkle, shipwrecked on No Man's Land for seven long and idle years.'

They had all heard rumours of my ordeal and wanted genuinely to hear details of it. I set out before them the bare essentials and, as a result, a dozen or more invitations were extended to me. The men were all masters of ships, older men of means and proprietors of large thriving sugar plantations with many slaves.

Each of them immediately donated a sum of money to help me with the expenses of rehabilitating myself to a life of ease and comfort, until such time as my letters reached England and my family could send me money. In less time than it took to tell, I watched my purse rise to the sum of five hundred pounds. On my way home, I came upon John who had been my kind companion on board the sloop. He had already heard of Yarico's outrageous and defiant behaviour.

'Poor child,' he said. 'Poor heathen child. Acted in a fit of devilry. A sailor I know has promised to let her swim if she could, when close to her island. I'm sure he'll let her go. She wouldn't last long in slavery.'

I nodded. How wonderful it would be if she could get away! But what of the sharks! I pushed her plight from me. I, too, had to survive and could not do so whilst imagining Yarico in shark-infested waters.

With the passing of time I became more and more a member of the island community. My good looks and comparative youth and my ordeal among the Caribs made me the recipient of motherly care from those women who had lost their sons to war or adventure in foreign parts. One of the women who could easily have been my mother, so alike she was in manner and nature, was Lady Sybil De Vere. Although imperious and self-assured, she readily placed youth at ease in her presence.

Her authority was like a tide approaching, its waters concealing every rock of doubt, every stone of uncertainty. She spoke up for the right way and was intolerant of the devious. Her round face, blooming cheeks, clustering chestnut curls and merry brown eyes composed a woman who had enjoyed all that was good in life without a care or concern for its procurement.

At our first meeting she sensed my insecurities and, seating me in an armchair in her parlour, poured me tea, all the while smiling as if she was sharing a confidence with the teapot.

'Now take your tea,' she said. 'And then tell me what you did on No Man's Land for seven long years.'

What could I do in the face of such a command but tell her truly of my life in the land of the Black Caribs?

'Of course they are different, but in their own land they believe that their way is the fit and proper way. They are close to the beasts of the field and imitate them in all things.'

Lady Sybil pondered my words momentarily, and then begun turning them over, seeking all that was savage and heathenish about the Caribs. Imagining the worst she could, she rained curses upon the creatures until little droplets of angry sweat marked her brow.

I moved over and took her hand.

'My Lady,' said I, 'we English are a proud and stubborn race. The evil of the Caribs, varied though it was, had little effect upon me.'

She smiled understandingly, all hatred of the heathen dissipated for a moment. She rose to greet her husband, Sir Harry, who had quietly entered the room. He bowed stiffly to me. He was a man whose face changed expressions with an amazing frequency. He served as an aide to His Excellency the Governor, and it was whispered that Sir Harry kept his eye upon the French, who were as devious and subterranean as the English, with regard to their territories in that part of the world. He was an elderly man, older by far than his wife, a man of fifty or thereabouts, and I could ascertain from the way he caressed her face with his eyes, small beneath an overhanging brow, that he truly loved her. She, though, from the evidence of the barely perceptible frowns and shrugs she made as Sir Harry expressed his liberal views concerning slavery and slaves, did not see eye to eye with her husband. It was then that I resolved my position concerning slavery. I did not agree with him.

He excused himself to attend to the affairs of the plantation and to visit his fine stable of horses; and after some more conversation I returned to Dunbar's where I was at that time still comfortably ensconced.

At last letters arrived from England. My brother Jonathan wrote with the sad, but not unexpected, news that both my parents were dead. Adam was in Virginia but of Alice there was complete silence. Once, she had been sighted on a plantation in Jamaica. It was said that she had been helping to propagate the Gospel among white settlers and plantation owners. Some time later she had been seen in England, and then there was no further information.

The letters also brought proof of my title to the family estates. These, Jonathan confirmed, were in better shape than they had been at the time of my original voyage. My brother Adam, who made the inspection that I had been on my way to carry out, had taken the estate out of the hands of a cheating attorney and replaced the former chief overseer with an industrious and honest man. I might, though, Jonathan suggested, by the encouragement of my presence, further improve the estate's efficiency and profitability. At the least, I could in time enjoy a comfortable living from it. In short, brother Jonathan wished me to stay in Barbados.

I was cast-down by the news and felt as exposed and lost as I had been in my sojourn among the heathens. What did I know of business, let alone the trade in sugar and the management of slaves? What, though, was there to look forward to in England? I resolved to do as my brother wished.

But before I could sink into a self-pitying state, Dunbar and his cronies had raced into the grounds, the hoofs of their horses like thunderclaps and their voices in raucous flow:

'I love my slave,
I love my wife.
A whip I use to love my slave
And gems to love my wife.
I love my slave,
I love my wife,
'Tis gems I give to love my wife
And naught to love my slave.'

It was a most disreputable song, which everyone applauded instead of taking umbrage at the words.

'Heed well that ditty.' Dunbar warned. 'For it is truly so. Men all over the world would say, "By Satan, 'tis so!"' It was at this point I discovered that I was stricken with shyness when in company. I grew very red and felt extremely confused, indeed so much so that my tongue was like lead in my mouth.

Shyness came upon me at any time, even when I rode about Dunbar's plantation with the dragoneer, an unyielding man, greatly feared by the slaves.

I was so preoccupied with my own predicament that it never occurred to me to ascertain the real cause of the slaves' fear in his presence. This was his practice of putting charms and fetishes about their houses and so controlling them. Remembering Paiuda's terror of fetishes and the people's fear of them, I did not care even to be within a sword's length of them. Some of the most docile slaves and the most beauteous to behold pandered to this overseer, but to me their colour proved an insurmountable barrier, for they reminded me of Yarico wholly or in part and she, like a dark shadow, haunted me. Sometimes I could not speak even to the servants, so fearful I was of her power and the mystery of her power. Had I not seen it with my own eyes that the life of the vital organs could be hindered by witchcraft? I bared my heart and soul to Dunbar and he, seeing that I was still far from ready to strike out on my own, redoubled his efforts to help me. He daily took me riding and to horseback games. The more competent

I became and the more people I met, the more I regained confidence in myself. I accepted many invitations to dine and soon was able to ride unaccompanied to Lady Sybil's each day to breakfast with her, Sir Harry and their circle of friends. Talk flowed freely at such gatherings and gossip ran ahead of discretion. There was no hiding place for news of any kind. I was now once more in the world and felt ready to take up residence on my estate.

Indeed, at breakfast one morning, I began to resent my position as an object of both nods of pity and whispers of sympathy. Everyone treated me with undue courtesy and care, the kind of care that was lavished upon expensive and fragile porcelain.

'Why am I being so cossetted?' I asked Lady Sybil. 'I can now accept my station once more.'

'Your news has not lately been good, has it, Mr. Inkle?'

'No. And its yield has been plentiful, like a good cane-field.'

She smiled faintly. 'Such amusing talk! Of course, your parents are in heaven! They must be.'

'Mama surely is. She was an angel to her family and her friends.'

'And your papa?'

'He had his devil-days. I trust he was given remission.'

She looked at me seriously. 'The devil is not to be joked about. As God is amongst us, so is the devil.'

I shrugged. 'The worry is, where is Alice? Somewhere between life and death? A dream! A shadow?'

'We will discover her location. Let us place our thoughts among the flowers and forget both devils and Alice.'

Round and round the gardens we walked, creating coils and mazes of silence, but at last her zest collapsed and we found a seat among some colourful shrubs that offered a view of the duck-pond and the trees screening the slave cabins. It was the first time I had been able to comprehend the beauty and magnitude of the place with its ponds and streams, screens and banks of flowers, stately palms, cannonball trees, almond and mahogany trees.

After a while I galloped into town. It was two o'clock and the men would all be dining at their clubs. If I did not join them I would have to wait the four hours before I could tell Dunbar of an idea that had come to me with the suddenness of lightning.

After dinner some of the men visited the houses of dubious pleasure, while others went home to their families. Before Dunbar could disappear, I blurted out my plans.

'I am going into the business of antiquities and fine furniture,' I said. 'I know so little of sugar that I must occupy myself in a trade of which I have some knowledge. Our overseer has managed the estate well enough these past seven years.

'Well done, old fellow,' he replied cheerfully. 'Now, why didn't I think of that? First you must get yourself a warehouse or two. That's essential.'

'I hadn't thought of that,' I said. 'Do you know of any empty warehouses?'

'As a matter of fact, I do. Donald Butcher has one coming up for auction soon. I'll bid as well to make sure you get it.'

Such a handy bit of scheming, I learned, paid dividends. I secured the admirably appointed warehouse and, with a few alterations and the sweat of knowledgeable slaves, I turned it into an elegant saleroom. It was a monumental task: the planning, figuring, letter-writing and reclaiming my lost knowledge of antiquities all led me down different avenues.

Lady Sybil and her coterie of inquisitive friends were my stalwart advisers, alerting me to those places where marital bliss was about to founder and gifts of appeasement a necessity. They further helped by playing on the vanities of gullible women by suggesting what was *à la mode* and what *passé* in the line of furniture.

Remembering my father's observations upon a trade in which his experience had been wide and deep provided extra guidance as well. Time and again I had heard him expound upon the foibles of men.

'Vanity, my son, and the desire for singularity move men to extravagance.'

This proved to be true, and as time passed I grabbed at Dame Fortune's petticoats and bound them to my future.

The business occupied all my time. I travelled extensively over the parishes to plantation sales acquiring beautiful objects. I had moved into the family plantation house in St James. It was an elegant house, though neglected, and I set about making it a place of profound beauty and peace. It became in time a showplace for the eyes of the covetous, the self-indulgent and the acquisitive.

My chief overseer ruled with a firm hand and I followed his example. Slaves were mercilessly punished for any insubordination and so the estate was immaculate. Everybody worked hard — men, women and children, the women fusing fertility with maternity to extend our stock. Gradually, I learnt much about the stamina of various tribes of slaves, and about avoiding those that were considered intractable, aggressive or given to rebellion. Plantation policy was to discard the aged and replenish with young; and it mattered not to me what the overseer did with those slaves who were worth nothing to us. The Society for the Propagation of the Gospel in Foreign Parts had plantations on the island and they rescued slaves discarded by others. They never branded their slaves.

My position now encouraged others to see me as rich and respectable rather than as having been tainted by my sojourn among cannibals, which the Caribs were truly thought to be. Indeed, I railed against those calumnies, but had no argument to counter words such as, 'If Caribs did not feast upon you, that says nought about their feasting upon us.'

In the end I gave up defending the Caribs against such beliefs. My people needed to think evil of those in circumstances different to theirs.

Apart from the young women of rank, quality and bourgeois expectations, there was another class of women — mulattoes and those indentured servants who had served their time and were determined to win independence for themselves. These women could be obtained for pleasure at bars, inns and taverns. The most popular *rendez-vous* of all at that time was a tavern in the centre of town, run by a wealthy half-African woman, Mary Bella Greene. She had travelled abroad with her master who, after his death, left her secure, free and independent. She had returned to the island and, rather than being stoned as a whore, had been allowed to cater for the needs of libertines, rakes and adventurers who visited this most English of islands.

Dunbar organised my first visit to the tavern where groups of men, all white, drank spirits served mainly by garrulous, rosy-cheeked wenches and inscrutable half-African women, who were famous for their beauty. Some of the women were rented out by their white masters for a lucrative fee. Among the clientele that night were ships' captains, some visiting gentlemen, rakes and sharpers who awaited their turns. To these men, a woman could be of any race or class, provided she was comely and could tenderly indulge their various vices.

To tell the truth, I approached the whole enterprise nervously and my anxiety increased during the long drive to the door. Inside, I observed that it had once been an elegant house. We entered the parlour, a kind of throne room where Mary Bella was ensconced. The soft furnishings were made softer and more luxurious by the flickering candlelight, and their sedate and speculative golds, greens and yellows seemed to give bones to familiarity and banish hesitancy. Mary Bella's smile came in flashes. She was a handsome young woman whose face was like a series of pictures that changed as moods and thoughts changed. Her brown hair swept back from a wide forehead and fell in a shower of writhing curls along her back. Enigmatic eyes emphasised the clear curves of mouth and nose.

It was said that men adored Mary Bella. Indeed, Dunbar kissed her heartily and then whispered, 'Bettina. Is it possible?' The head moved a mere whisker and the deed was done. Most discreetly, he presented me. 'Inkle is not an initiate,' said he calmly. 'See that he is indulged. He is extremely shy. Can you cure him of it?'

'A drink? Some ale, Mr Inkle?'

I declined. She could observe my nervousness — my twitching fingers, my gathering brows.

'A fruit-posset perhaps?'

I nodded.

'You would enjoy an evening with Delvina. Like yourself, not an initiate.' She clapped her hands and Delvina, a dark-haired girl, came promptly through the slit in the curtain. She brought an abundance of gaiety, laughter and fun with her in her movements, the toss of her head and the merry twinkle in her eyes. No great beauty, but surely a well-proportioned girl with a pear-shaped face, autumn-apple cheeks, a dimpled chin and a rather large nose. She curtsied to me and with that I heard the swish of the satin she wore. I had very slowly become able to accept the bulk of clothing worn by my people, especially women.

'Well now, let us see. What shall we do? It is helpful to have some pleasant conversation. So go ahead and ask me whatever comes into your head — anything at all.'

'Have you been long in this beautiful country?'

'No, no. I was taken on board ship against me will. Helping a creature, I was! The harridan pleaded with me and while I was fussing with her children, the ship put out to sea and there I was in the middle of the ocean.'

'You could have swum to shore.'

'I could not. I could say naught to anyone from her heaving and spewing all over me, from the movement of the ship. Then in a day or two she ups and dies. So there I was left with him and their children. None cared about their mother, dead and gone to her creator.'

I told her a bit of my adventures and then asked, 'Why didn't you insist that the gentleman take care of you?'

'Who — the preacher? He took up with a sickening woman who's now making slaves of his children. This woman also produced forged papers to show that she had hired me to serve five years, so I ends up here earning money to which he lays full claim.'

'So you have to deliver up your earnings?'

She nodded. 'He gets the money — him and her — and I work like a slave. I like to go for one gentleman who must make it worth my while. I don't like this life. I will sing to you. I'll get my lute.'

As she strummed, she sang in the middle range a song that told of an old couple's fate:

'Coyly she stood and so did he,
There beneath the linden tree.
Come, my love, a measure we'll tread
To mark the sixtieth year we wed.
Oh dear me! Oh dearie, dearie me!
My poor old heart still yearns for thee!
The fiddler came, aye so did he,
Underneath the linden tree.
He found some merry tunes to play
Same as on their wedding day.
Oh dear me! Oh dearie dearie me!
My poor old heart still yearns for thee.
The devil came and snipped the line
That river of love that flowed like wine
And she sat down and rose no more
For she had lived to be four score.
Oh dear me! Oh dearie dearie me!
My poor old heart still yearns for thee.'

It was a beautiful song. I kissed her hand and then took her in my arms and kissed her warmly. I then sat her on my lap and began to talk softly to her, telling her of my deep loneliness and of my love for some woman yet to be found. After these words the warmth in my heart died away and my physical ardour also. 'Love is the finest thing in the world, is it not?' said I.

'Yes, love is. It requires time to ripen, does it not? What I receive is neither love nor regard.'

I could not disagree.

'Then we must await a hearty feast, Sir, but sadly someone else does not think so. Therefore, here I am, at your will.'

'I think with deep affection of you. I came here upon a good purse and will cover your charge.'

'Will you return?'

'Of course, with an eager expectation.' My shyness vanished. I bade her a peaceful night and God speed and left Mary Bella's ahead of Dunbar.

When later I dined with Sybil, I was careful not to brag or even to hint of my adventure at Mary Bella's, yet all the while I wondered if she had guessed. Two of her young widowed friends were present, one a sour woman who was engaged upon a crusade to find a younger and richer husband than her deceased, and Anne, who was sweet, fashionable and self-contained. I drank tea with them. We were merry and then went for a carriage drive in the country. The plantation houses, some built in the Greek style, sat plump and sleek and cossetted by riotous flowers. The most stately trees stood in their grounds and filled my heart with joy, for they showed to me the clear meaning of civilisation. All the while Anne sat silent and contemplative, though I spent my time wondering how she would look in a natural state in the forest, and whether or not it would be a sweet encounter to make love to her.

'Pray, Anne,' I said. 'Don't be so much upon ceremony. Smile! Life can be full of joy.'

'I trust so, Tommy. Sometimes I cannot command my spirits. I am thinking of Louise, for she has found a Frenchman in Tobago, just by chance.'

'In time, good lady, you will too. I know that it is now hard. Will he wed her or simply bed her?'

'Both, it would appear,' and she laughed like a person in pain.

I could think of nothing else all week but my vow to return to Delvina. I did not, though, disclose my path to Dunbar, for he would have made sport of me and mocked my constancy.

On the appointed day I returned to Mary Bella's in a

vigorous frame of mind. Delvina at once came to me and I sat her down and began toying with her.

'Oh Sir, so soon,' she complained. 'This is very hard, Sir, I am frightened. There are distracting tales told about you. And are you still shy? I must not confuse you.'

'There is too much talk in this place,' said I. 'You poor creature, to have your ears so tortured by tales. You must call upon me and then I will prove to you that there is nothing to be feared. And as for my shyness, it has melted away like morning dew.'

I suggested that we should dine together and was very hearty about the matter. I liked her company. She was quite without malice or pretence. She confessed prettily to using guile to find handsome company, without in the least seeming worldly. She was most agreeable and when we returned to her room she sat upon my knee and told me amusing tales of her home, her family and their life on the edge of the law.

I took stock of my purse. I had contributed two sizeable sums of money and still had not been able to satisfy my desires. I therefore arranged with Mary Bella that my carriage should collect Delvina and convey her to my plantation to have tea with me. My excitement was like a birdsong, high-pitched and articulate at the prospect of this sweet assignation. I made meticulous preparations for the visit, my slaves laying out a lavish repast. At the named hour Delvina arrived. I could see that she was quite overcome by the splendour in which I lived.

'I am quite in a flutter,' she said. 'I never could have imagined such a place. I feel a poor flower-seller in such surroundings.'

It pleased me that she was confounded. She had dressed tastefully, her same childish vivacity in place, and she was now in my possession. When we were alone I embraced her warmly and pleaded with her not to delay my urge. When we entered the bedroom, though, she declined to undress in my presence.

'Madam, your body is your own. Delight in it. Do not be unenamoured of it.'

Later I came like a shadow into the room, slid into the bed and embraced her. After all the dalliance, she was mine. Uncomfortable though it was to be above her, I was able 'to laugh with her' so that my blood raced through my veins to end in supreme rapture. Papa would have said, 'If you cannot have what you want, then want what you have.'

We took tea afterwards and then indulged yet again until darkness, like a gentle blanket, enfolded us. Next morning, the early sunshine streaming into the room woke us up and I once more pressed my suit, but this time to no avail.

'I shall be whipped, I am sure of it,' she said. 'What a loss my last night's earnings shall be to the hawk, my master, and the shark, Mary Bella.'

'Set your heart at ease,' said I. 'You will, by my stalwart help, buy your freedom from your oppressors. While you embark upon a more benign path, my home will offer you both shelter and respite, if absolute secrecy is maintained.'

I was, though, so enamoured of Delvina that I publicly took her on a visit to one of my valued customers. Here I discovered the pitfalls of *my* lack of discretion.

We walked up the path to the house, watched by slaves weeding and hoeing the extensive gardens. Why did each one of us need so much land? Delvina, wearing a saucy hat a-top her curls, a dress with a full, blowing skirt and gleaming black boots bustled around the garden. The footman took my card and hastened to present it. Delvina could not resist the butterflies and tried to capture some, albeit without a net. I pointed out the uselessness of her efforts.

'You'll be kilt,' she shouted. 'You brute of an Englishman. The curse of Satan upon you for callin' me useless.' She placed a finger in a fountain of the water gardens and then a whole hand as she savoured the sensation of cold water.

My hostess appeared and was so overcome by the brashness before her that she ignored Delvina's curtsy.

'Out of me way, y'ould crow. 'Tis snobbery that will kill you. Tell 'im to wed me and put me in an aisy frame of mind and I shall be as good as you.'

'Who is this creature, Tommy? How could you insult me so?'

I apologised to sweet Olivia and vowed never more to visit accompanied by 'a member of my family'. Later I confided the adventure to Lady Sybil and discovered that hatred of the lower classes, who arrived as indentured servants, was rife.

'Is she of the Irish race?'

'I have not ascertained. But if she is called Delvina O'Hara, I expect her father was.'

'Good Lord! A peasant papist in our midst! Unheard of! I am a Christian, sir, and I would not have allowed her in my door.'

'I will not bring her among you.'

'Very well, see that you do not. For they seek to better their lot through scheming and concubinage.'

'She is but a youth! A mere flower. Free of twists and turnings.'

'Papists, young or old, are dangerous. Harry knows these truths and even a cursory look at reports will convince you of it.'

She sipped her tea carefully.

'When I was a mere gal, my uncle, who fought the causes of Turks, if I recall correctly, brought one into the house. "No, no!" said my nurse — for my mother had died and she guarded my every waking moment. "He cannot sleep here. We are Christians and should not offer a bed to a heathen." He slept on the floor in the summer house. I worried that he would die of cold but he was up at the crack of dawn drinking tea and eating hot muffins with great gusto.'

Christianity seemed each day to mean less in that place, but I assured her that whatever she did then, she was as good as an angel now. She smiled warmly at me and pressed my hand.

CHAPTER SIX

I was not to hear the last from Lady Sybil of my indiscretion with Delvina. Throughout luncheon she continued to scold me, between mouthfuls, for associating with the lower classes.

'What have the Caribs done to you!' she chided, 'How could you choose with such ease women of low degree?'

I, though, throughout the two hours of luncheon and throughout her scoldings, thought only of Delvina, who like Zeze, my youthful delight, contained a mixture of devilry and sobriety which rendered her mercilessly compelling to me. I imagined Delvina nibbling my ear and whispering sweet and charming endearments to me. Pleasure flooded over me like sunshine, and I was reminded of some lines I had read in Mr Shakespeare's *Troilus and Cressida*.

'Fie, fie upon her!
There's language in her eye, her cheek, her lip,
Nay, her foot speaks; her wanton spirits look out
At every joint and motive of her body.'

Later I attended at my office in Bridgetown and arranged several pressing matters, and was intent upon undertaking more when dear Anne, with her slave carrying purchases, called at my salesroom. I made my pleasure at seeing her clear. After exchanging pleasantries, our talk turned to the rumours of cruelties to slaves.

'Do you know of it, Tommy? I know not of it!' she remarked in a spirited manner. 'My slaves do as they please, except for the vigilance of the "jumpers" and their whips.'

'I have heard tell of the barbarity of their capture,' said I.

'But Africans enjoyed their barbarity well before our arrival upon the shores of the dark continent. They are not blameless in the capture and sale of their people. They prepare impenetrable forts to hold them prisoner and then… well, they sell them to whoever offers better trinkets. There is no such thing as families among them. The tribe exists but the family does not. Enough, sweet Anne. Trouble yourself not about such perfidy. 'Twould be more entertaining to view the latest arrival of silver fancies from home.'

She made several purchases and left in her chaise to visit other establishments.

At that time of the afternoon, the more respectable taverns were full of men eager to talk politics or business or discuss the vagaries of trade. Having no mind for such talk, I drove my carriage home to Delvina. The horses, unhappy at the heat, refused to be hurried. When at last I arrived she seemed quite content, having spent most of the morning, as she confessed, singing and titivating herself. There was a hint of indifference in her voice and, thinking that her ardour for me had diminished, I enquired after her happiness, her desires and her contentment.

She replied that all was to her approval, then added, 'You have a gilded cage, Sir, and I do not consider myself the bird to be kept in it. I will not be caged, Sir. I love freedom far too much.'

It was as if I had been wilfully pricked by a thorn. I thought of my time with the Caribs and of my need of freedom. I at once set aside the east wing for Delvina's use, with her own slaves to tend her and obey her on pain of death. Grateful though she was, she declined my special considerations, saying that she had but made me aware of her innermost feelings, and spoken her mind. She later permitted me the tenderest rites of love, which greatly uplifted my spirits. I lay beside her recovering from the discomfiture of bedclothes, the walls of the house itself, the distraction of voices, the presence of furniture and all the remains of civilisation, when she remarked that Dunbar had not only called whilst I was out at my office, but that she had gone horseback riding with him. She chuckled softly to herself.

'I ran alongside his horse. It amused the slaves. Running against a horse is hard work. How do they do it?'

I was furious. I knew Dunbar as a lecherous card, and I imagined the leering looks he gave my love, his suggestive comments, his brash touches.

'Madam,' I said, 'you seem to caper around like a bitch in season. Mr Dunbar will certainly bed you, but never wed you.' She laughed up the very storm of a laugh.

'Do I hear the green-eyed monster roaring? When I was a nursemaid to the preacher's children he walked hand-in-hand with it. It pulled the tears from my eyes, as is being done now.' And she laughed again.

Her displeasure, though, was transient, and a wonderful supper of roast beef and vegetables revived us so much that I demonstrated natural scenes from Carib life so that she could savour the simple pleasures of a simple people.

It was a welcome sight each day to observe my saleroom crowded with men from the neighbouring islands. Their purses heavy from the sale of their sugar, they delighted in buying little trinkets such as a carved table or an expensive canvas for their estate. I had installed, also, a portrait painter, a capable Jew from the island of Martinique. He produced a ready silhouette or a charcoal likeness for a fee, to the delight of these ignorant rich men.

My business had its amusing side too, for I quite frequently found myself selling and then reselling the same articles as the local fashions in furniture and pictures changed. To add variety and create new horizons of greed in my customers I decided to travel to neighbouring lands in search of rarer objects. Santa Lucia, being then neutral and loved by both the French and the English, seemed a likely place to visit.

I had appointed three capable assistants to help me in the warehouse and the showrooms, so there was no problem with travel in respect to carrying on my business. My one concern was that I had assumed the care of Delvina, after generously paying Mary Bella for her release into my protection. I hesitated to entrust her to my friend, Mr. Dunbar, and far from being able to call on the help of any of my women friends, I had to conceal the depth of my association with her from both Lady Sybil and Anne, who pressed me sorely to consider having a wife to grace my table. From the ardour with which she spoke, I suspected that Anne considered herself the perfect wife for me. But I was already spoken for, albeit by Delvina. Really, I never once thought to express tender sentiments to Anne. I never thought of love in her presence. She was a woman who did not need anything as silly or trivial as love.

On our next drive around her estate I told her of my impending visit to Santa Lucia.

'There is great animosity between our people and the French. It was rumoured that they poisoned a well, so that Britons would die.'

'Oh fie,' said I, 'the slaves did it. And then the Caribs did it. Then the missionaries themselves. 'Twas said they all did it turns about.'

'You will do well to take care. But talking of Santa Lucia, they possess the most beauteous child-slaves for sale.'

I had never interested myself in such matters but I knew that the children were sold in 'parcels' of twenty to thirty, when aged between five and eight, much as sheep were bought in England.

'When is the sale to be held?'

'In a week's time. I need a child and you could help me to get a good one. I want one, very black. Not sickly. One that would enhance my porcelain vases.'

Anne had a most disarming manner. She saw dread in every enterprise or adventure and then, as if to reassure herself, she added an errand to it. I promised to buy her a child-slave as soon as I could.

My anxiety about leaving Delvina at home was justified. When I returned from Santa Lucia I found her greatly angered.

'You have forgotten. It is the King's birthday tomorrow and it is to be celebrated with songs at Mary Bella's. You have forgotten! There were letters come to remind you. There is also to be a fine ball.'

I confessed that I had forgotten all about the ball, though the truth was that such occasions bewildered me and I had decided that whether I displeased society or not, whether I displeased Delvina or not, I would not attend. I could not face the crowd, the false courtesies, the protocol. The thought alone made me feel disagreeable.

'There would be no welcome for you at the ball, my dear,' said I, 'so there will be none for me. I am here now and we could spend the time more agreeably together.'

'Will we?' she asked, like a child robbed of a sweetmeat. I caressed her hair, and then with a great hunger enjoyed her. I must have fallen asleep for when I awoke she had gone. I stood by the window listening to the quiet murmurings of the slaves in the moonlight. Was she out there with them, talking, trying to make friends with them and by her efforts terrifying them? She was not. What I took to be her skirt was only some material, washed and hanging, billowing out in the wind. I then discovered that her few possessions had also been taken. She had returned to her old haunts, I supposed, and with a very angry heart I vowed never to see her again.

I had learned among the Caribs to control my anger, for it did no good to show it, and so went about my business as though all was well. Anne and Sybil both talked with enthusiasm about the splendid ball, and I explained yet again the bewildering effect upon me of gatherings and other splendid occasions.

Later that evening I felt a burning sensation, followed by a throbbing pain in my member. The pain soon became a discharge. What was to be done? Were my bones and blood decaying before my eyes? Oh the thought of it! Perhaps I had hurt myself in my haste to love Delvina? Was I at the mercy of the heat of the tropics? The next day brought a recurrence of the symptoms. I sorely needed someone in whom I could confide. My suffering was now mental as well as physical.

I despatched a message to Dunbar, who hastened to my side. I poured my symptoms into his ears.

He winked. 'My young friend,' he said, 'you have had a visit from my Lord Gonorrhoea. Your last lady friend — whoever it was — has bequeathed it to you. Think hard. Who was it?'

I did not need to think hard. I had never been in such an arrangement with other than Delvina, and I could not countenance it to be a deliberate act on her part. But Dunbar insisted.

'She knows you will not marry her. She knows you are of some substance. Therefore she leaves her mark upon you. You will need a physician and his discretion as well as his skill will have to be recompensed. I know one such fellow. We will not deal in names.'

The physician, an admirable man, examined me carefully. 'The disease has not yet taken hold. You will need to be a month or more under my hand and I must inform you it will be an expensive cure.'

'Tell me, would the young woman be aware of such symptoms and deliberately use me ill?' I asked.

'It is unlikely that the symptoms would be unknown to her. That would be miraculous. A harridan, Sir! A dissembling whore! I see so much of this vile behaviour.'

Had I been face to face with Delvina at that moment I would have certainly insulted her most severely, but perhaps the fact that she was now in some unknown place proved the better thing.

Dunbar, discreet and confidential, kept me well disposed during the long weeks of my treatment. When I was cured, I resolved never again to visit a tavern, an inn or a whorehouse, or journey down such risky paths.

Anne was a devoted friend and companion all through this time of anguish, though the true nature of my illness was kept from her. She daily showed her unselfishness, her goodness and her charity. She spoke upon the most serious of subjects and always ended up smiling sweetly. I could not, though, help but find in her a rigid narrow-mindedness. She reminded me of those forest-plants that shrivelled and died, even though there was sufficient air, water and food available for them. I thought often to marry her but knew that at close quarters we might cause each other pain.

These reflections and Delvina's perfidy led me to feel that it was time to think about returning to England. I would undertake a grand tour of the islands, starting with Santa Lucia, collect new antiquities and pictures from them, sell them at a good price in Barbados, and return to England a rich man. There I would search diligently for Alice and discover her fate once and for all. I would also, joyfully and sadly, pay my respects to the graves of my poor parents. Then, at last, I could untie the knots of pain and grief that lay so deeply in my heart.

I was still haunted by memories of Delvina. I was undoubtedly a most unlucky man in the affairs of the heart. Alice, Yarico, Zeze to whom I made love by the soft light of fireflies, and Delvina, who seized me like a fire in brushwood. All gone from me. I placed my fears before Dunbar but he dismissed them as inflicting doubt, the worst of the vices, upon myself.

'I married an heiress,' he said. 'We do not love. She is happy in Georgia and I am deliriously occupied here. When perchance we meet, we act our parts. She the devoted wife and I the doting husband. My heavens, how very tormenting the whole performance.'

The dry season had arrived and the time of storms, hurricanes and rumbustious winds had passed, and so, without further wavering, I once again boarded a cutter for Santa Lucia to meet with a potential new seller. He was Dr John Clarkson who lived with his family on Woodenridge plantation just outside Castries.

As I drove into the town with its French and English-style architecture, the mists of the river gave way to a cloudless, brilliant blue sky with the mountains of Souffriere blue-grey and elemental in the distance. The gardens, tended by slaves, were full of flowers spanning the colours of the rainbow against the dark green of towering hardwood; with palm trees cutting into the valleys, the island was like a ridged fabric.

The view of the Bay of Castries, now behind me, showed a natural harbour, crowded with shipping and surrounded by houses like eggs in a nest. Above them the slowly turning windmills, cannonball trees, the soft murmuring of doves and the trilling of song birds added their own mystery. Escaped slaves frequently made Santa Lucia their first stop on the road to freedom and hid in maroonage there.

The carriage stopped outside an elegant house showing all the signs of change of ownership and I made haste to the door to shake hands with Dr John Clarkson, with whom my business lay.

The slave, a footman in faded livery, informed me in halting French, and then in splendid English, that Dr Clarkson had not yet returned from the factory to which he had been summoned, but that he would acquaint his mistress of my presence. I entered a pretty room with much of the furnishings on the point of being removed. The door opened and an elegant woman entered. I surely had seen the face before but could not recollect where. When she spoke, apologising for her husband's absence, her voice informed me as to her identity. I was dumbfounded. It was as if a sword had been thrust into me. Alice stood before me.

'I am Thomas Inkle, Madam, and English like yourself.' She pretended not to recognise me. I could see her rapidly trying to decide upon a course. But all to no avail. She confusedly tried to mouth my name but was silent. Pale as water and trembling like a palm frond in the wind, she stood in a state of deep shock. Silence hung in the air, confounding the moment. She seemed to be in another world.

'Ah, Mr Inkle,' said a voice from behind me. 'Forgive my absence. I see, however, you have met my wife. I am a physician as well as a planter and am sometimes caught between the two stools.'

I smiled weakly. He crossed the room, shook hands with me and turned to present his wife, but she staggered, then fell at his feet.

'Oh, my dear! My dear!' Clarkson cried anxiously, gathering her up and calling for help. 'Not one of your turns again?'

He carried her up the stairs and into her chamber. He soon returned and with some complacency said, 'My wife gets these turns now and again. She was greatly shocked once. Her betrothed was lost at sea. Mercifully she recovers very quickly. Two drops of sal volatile sniffed and the blood flows once more to her head.'

I was calm outside but a hurricane raged in my entrails, almost uprooting every vestige of self-control. For a moment I looked helplessly in her direction, trying to recall all those words that down the passing years I had intended to tell her. I recalled the crescent of her mouth in such wonderful harmony with her face and the clear green of her eyes and thought, 'My Alice — so near and yet so far — and between us a bond that could not be rent asunder except by death, yet here we are in the presence of another life and another love.'

'My wife is once more herself and will be down if you would take tea with us,' he said simply.

I nodded. My Alice, now beyond Eros, since I could never reconquer what was lost.

'We are returning to England after a brief visit to the plantations around Bridgetown. We'll be the guests of the Codringtons' plantation. Besides, my work here is done.'

'I have heard that this island has been greatly agitated by the French navy,' I said.

'Not only are they heartless at sea. They are devils on land, especially to their slaves. No! This island must be in our hands. We must keep it, no matter how often they come!'

A battle seemed to be raging inside him, one which as an Englishman he could not afford to lose. I reminded him of the reason for my visit and helped by slaves to move the pieces of furniture, we viewed and priced them, some being of the most exquisite craftsmanship. The bell was rung for tea. A more sumptuous table I never saw, but my appetite had become misery and a wish for things to end. Alice, too, ate sparingly, though her colour was now restored. All she needed to say was, 'This is the man. He was not dead after all.' But she did not, fearing I suppose that such an admission could hold serious implications.

'Tell me, Mr Inkle, of your antiquities. Is it a delight each day to feast the eye upon old and beautiful things? Is that all you do?' she asked, reminding me that there had always been an element of the supercilious in her.

'I have slept under other skies, drunk from other springs and idled beneath trees that sheltered me from storms, Madam.' We sipped tea.

'Dearest,' said her husband, 'You must partake of Chloe's cake or she will be grossly displeased! And you too, Sir.'

Dutifully we obeyed and then, tea over, Alice suggested that I saw some furniture in the west wing of the house. The plantation seemed a well-run place. Children approached and jabbered at us without hostility. One little Carib boy called Tim, aged about nine, seemed a particular favourite. He was even allowed to carry a blowpipe around with him. I asked about him.

'I found him,' Alice explained, 'kidnapped and then abandoned for dead, but he killed the men with his blowpipe and will not be parted from it.'

'A spirited fellow,' added Clarkson. 'I must, however, leave my wife in your compassionate care. There is much to be done. If one is to understand the sickness of these poor creatures there is much to be done and the papers await my return to the library.'

As soon as he had gone, she turned upon me and fiercely said, 'Why did you come here? You knew that your presence would be mischievous.'

'I knew nothing of your existence on this earth, in this island. News came variously of your presence in India, in Jamaica, in China — as a missionary.'

'Nonsense. I heard of the loss of your ship and journeyed to Jamaica to seek information at first hand. It was a hardy voyage, but I met dear John who helped me at every turn and in every way to seek news of him whom my soul so dearly loved. And when we were assured of your death by the slave-boy Jimmy, who was brought to me, I married John.'

'Jimmy! What befell Jimmy?'

'Why, nothing terrible. He's here with us and sees to the welfare of the children. Do you wish to see him? He will be left here as part of the stock.'

'Oh well, there is scant place for sentiment. I learned so among the Black Caribs who held me captive for seven long years. They are still often with me still. Heavens, how I suffered! What agonies of heart and soul! Mercifully, you knew nothing of my pain.' My desire for her sympathy was like a salt taste in my mouth, like the damp wind blowing over the sea. She threw her arms about me in a gesture of compassion, perhaps of atonement, but I rebuked her and assured her of my true delight in her happy union.

'John is fine, right through to his blood and bones, kind and just and as clever a physician as has ever been born. His work is very pressing,' she said, her eyes loudly asserting her certainties.

'What work? You said yourself he is a physician.'

'But there is more. To reveal it would place us in the utmost jeopardy. Oh, the cruelties of the owners of this island! Men with hearts of stone!'

'Frenchmen?' I asked.

'And Dutch and English. And Portuguese. They are all the same in disregarding of the children of God. Oh, the travail of these times!'

After she had shown me the rest of the pieces they had to offer, I assured her that she should place the facts before her husband. If he was in truth the man she described, then honour would be served all round if she confided that I was lost and now was found.

She suggested we drove out to the sands at Migrie, a place of breathtaking beauty, though she warned, 'Great care must be taken when walking, for one comes suddenly upon deadly snakes.'

The whole island showed God's delicate artistry, but most worthy of praise were the wonderful mountains that changed colours throughout the day, which was darkening in a gentle, deliberate manner when we returned. There were many inns and taverns, but for want of company they pressed me to stay on as their guest. John talked mainly of the diseases that were peculiar to the slaves and I mainly of my experiences in the world of antiquities. When I began to talk of my father, Alice uttered a little cry and then, in the most theatrical manner, sobbed, 'Dear God, John, we searched in vain! Thomas Inkle was never lost at sea! This is he! The man for whom we sought so thoroughly. My betrothed!'

Silence — for many full minutes. After that time, embarrassment was set aside and I was able to talk freely of my shipwreck, the massacre of the crew and the bare elements of my life among the Caribs. I thanked John for so nobly protecting Alice and for devoting his life to her happiness. I assured him most solemnly of familial affection and then retired to the room assigned to me.

The deed was done! The ghost of the past had been laid to rest.

I spent just two more days on the island and afterwards the atmosphere changed to one of easy friendship and confidences as Alice and I walked in her beautiful grounds or drove to the sands.

She said, 'There is talk of the abolition of the curse of slavery. How do you stand on this issue?'

'I have never thought about the matter. I expect that there must be slaves. We've always had them to toil for us.'

'Tommy, if I place you upon an oath, if I put my life into your hands, will you betray it? Whatever happens, will you keep silent?'

I looked at her sternly and said, 'Upon my honour as an Englishman.'

'Well then,' she said, lowering her voice into a whisper. 'We are abolitionists. John's Uncle Thomas is, in England, a founder of the cause and under the physician's cloak we gather information attesting to the cruelties endured by slaves. We talk to ships' captains and others concerned with the trade and hope to place our information before the Members of Parliament and win, albeit in future years, the end of this vile trade.'

'So you practise deception!'

'In a good cause.'

'Against kith and kin who would be reduced to beggary?'

'In Christ there is no black or white. All men are brethren. That is right.'

'Oh, Alice! Alice! What is right is what keeps us in our separate places. We are a superior race. We need others lower than ourselves. Irish, Jews, slaves. In Barbados, Jews are forbidden to employ Irish servants. Irish folk work only in their own fields. That is the way. Put such ideas of abolition out to shrivel in the sun.'

'You must not betray my confidence! John will not forgive me. Are you too wealthy to care for the poor? Oh Tommy, do you remember when we were children, you gave your cake to the hungry Lascar?'

I could not remember. Tim, the Carib boy, came close, sniffing at me as if finding in me a smell previously known.

'Is he the only one you have here?' I asked, indicating him.

'Once, two or three years ago, we found a woman put on this island from a ship. She was in a sorry state, but we tended her and she returned to her island: No Man's Land. All the time she was here she never spoke, except to him. He said there were stories of sadness in her heart. We never learned her name or whence she had come. She was a beautiful woman, the colour of sapodillas. In the red material she wore around her shoulders she carried a piece of wood carved like a child. Sometimes she whispered a name but no one could decipher it.'

'A demented nymph in the green,' I remarked with a smile.

The following day I returned to Barbados, all the while wondering if the abolitionists would indeed come to our island and spy upon us so that laws could be passed against us by rich liberals in the House of Parliament. All through the journey I thought about ways in which I could foil them without causing Alice or her husband harm. Since I had sworn Alice's confidence, I could not share my knowledge with any of my planter friends. Among them were men whose raw hatred of those who sought to change their lucrative lives knew no bounds. Alice, after all, I could recall as a small girl coming to tea on a grey day and talking in a piping, squeaky, voice. Now she had changed from a frail girl into an adventurous woman with a cause. Compared to Anne and Sybil, she seemed full of something sturdier. Where they carried sap, she contained matter that had crystallised into causes, beliefs and convictions: resentment of injustice and hatred of slavery. But where would I have been without slavery? I wished that she would change, but her convictions were firm as iron; to try to talk them out of her would be like trying to catch the mist in the morning air.

There was nothing I could do to return her to that simple state which had encouraged my parents to choose her as my lifelong companion. She was gone from me and gone for ever. I could not love her. To love is to trust and of that there was none. To love is to share confidences, be at peace, return smile with smile and kiss with kiss. She and her husband kissed through their causes, through their prayers and through their ardent concern with the Abolition Movement—which would reduce good men to beggary.

CHAPTER SEVEN

The plantation was in good heart, yet I felt myself heavily burdened by it. In reality, the more I thought of things the more the whole island of Barbados, pleasant and generous in itself, became an oppression to me. Even as I walked away from the quay towards my carriage and passed among the indigent and the superannuated slaves, white beggars, deserters and vagabonds, all dependent on the charity of the rich, my spirit deepened into gloom as I recalled Alice's words.

'Freedom for them! They are our brethren!'

Christmas was approaching. It heralded a time of feasting and reflection upon the life of the Holy Family; the time when ships arrived with cargo and supplies of luxury and indulgence for the plantations; the time when, the crops harvested and in place, the work in the fields light, the slaves were rewarded with extra rations which brought them with a spurt to good health, and a desire to throw themselves into the celebrations of the feast of Christmas.

My gloom deepened when I learned from my chief overseer that a recently acquired parcel of stout Coromantin men had obtained rum from the household slaves by threatening them with the casting of spells, had made themselves very drunk, and punishment had been administered to the extent that one had died of it.

'Fie! Loathsome man!' I stormed at the overseer. 'Will you repay the cost of the creature? It is good money that you yield up to your excess. You will repay me!'

I sensed, too, much discontent from the surliness of my house-servants in their daily tasks, the cause of which I could not tell. Surely the work of abolitionists had not yet reached these parts! The island was English, had only ever been English, and we were a kind people to those who depended on us.

The saleroom was a place of easier heart. It was crowded with planters from the islands — Tobago, Grenada and Antigua among them — seeking pewter, pottery, silver and such like for their wives and their mistresses. The delivery of the purchases I had made from the French and British houses in Santa Lucia had been delayed, but I had high hopes for their instant sale on arrival in Barbados. When the work was lighter, I drove into the countryside with my mentor, Lady Sybil, and my cherished friend, Anne, who now suspected that Delvina had something to do with my previous indisposition. I wanted to explain everything, to confess. How I wished I could have spoken freely, as I would have done among the Caribs, where delicacy about such matters was unknown! A man freely discussed his problems, exposing himself to ridicule, support and comfort all at the same time. The gods and spirits of time and place, as well as the ancestors, would be invoked and his cure would be of communal concern. But like the triangular trade, affecting Africa, Barbados and England, my secret must be known only to myself, Dunbar and the physician. No one else must know of it.

We talked instead of Christmas and the way the slaves sought to celebrate this season.

'It is the time, Tommy, when you know if there is trust on your plantation,' Anne volunteered. 'The greater the trust, the more familiarity the slaves express. And you could be sure thereafter that trust would always keep you informed of plots and impending misdemeanours.'

'I have forbidden slaves entry into my home and that is how it will remain,' I said. 'I have no need for plantations, but the price of sugar is good and that is my reason for being a planter.'

The whole business of slavery did not much exercise my mind, except when I had to consider either expense or profit.

'It gives me some concern for humanity. But not the way

Harry thinks. He would let them all go free,' Sybil said wearily.

'Then we will have to carry them back to Africa again,' said Anne. 'And will they remember whence they came? Why put them to such trouble? Let us keep them, even if we occasionally have to chide them, albeit through our faithful "jumpers".'

We laughed happily at the straightforwardness of Anne's views.

'You must spend Christmas Day with me and Boxing Day with Sybil, so you can see for yourself their antics and cavortings and hear their barbaric music,' she continued.

I promised that I would not fail her.

I was still haunted by thoughts of Delvina. I had learned both from my father and from the Caribs to ponder only those dilemmas that affected me, and this was one. Until I received some explanation of her ill-usage of me, I would keep up my interest in her whereabouts.

That evening I ate alone, but my peace of mind was disturbed by an entertainment in the slave quarters. They were a good distance away from the main house and screened by lignum vitae, mahogany and silk-cotton, all very old and encircled by hardy shrubs and grass to form a clearing. The music, though muted, was a haunting bel-canto. It drew me outside and I noticed that the slaves wore masks and were in the act of performing a play. Curiosity compelled me to watch. It was a most amusing spectacle in which all those of us significant in the day-to-day running of plantation life were being caricatured. Dancing, they approached me and I was so well pleased with their exhibition that, on the spot, I offered them extra rations. They were well pleased and wholehearted in their good wishes. I, relieved to see the happy smiles on their faces, now free of the hideous masks, left them to their clowning.

When I returned to the house I found a letter which had been left on the doorstep. I opened it and found to my perturbation that Delvina had at last contacted me. She said little, but included an address among her few, meagre sentences. I was thrown into turmoil and retired immediately to my bed where guilt, shame and anxiety all ruthlessly tortured me. I dreamed of Yarico dressed in sunlight, its soft folds about her brown-gold body, her mass of hair a noose about my neck. I dreamt that the *infusoria* that Delvina had bequeathed to me had become substantial men, some with faces like my customers, threatening to gibbet me. To save myself, I had hidden in a large silver dish and lay curled up like a terrified foetus in it. As I struggled to put the lid in place, along came Alice who securely contained me in it. It then became transparent and I could not help but notice the satisfaction on her face as she said, 'He will do us no harm here, John, he must surely die.' And pointing at me, John said solemnly, 'I am the resurrection and the life, saith the Lord: he that believeth in me, though he were dead, yet shall he live and…'

I woke up.

Before the sun rose, I set out to find Delvina. Her address was in a parish which was the haunt of the indentured classes. It was perhaps a foolhardy thing to do, but I could not help myself.

The 'housemistress' admitted me and pointed the way to the rooms at the top of the stairs. It seemed a good class of household.

'I see before me a fine English gentleman,' said the lady of the house, her energies in full flood as she thumped and thudded up the stairs. 'Irish or English?' she asked.

'I am English.'

Smiling broadly, she added, 'Now I am t'inkin' how did a fine man like you let such a turrible fate befall you?'

'Madam, I can assure you it is not such a bad fate, except to those who cannot be English.'

'Well, we will talk about that another day, but Miss O'Hara may be found in these quarters — her and her airs and graces.'

I knocked upon the door and Delvina, as fresh and desirable as a roast goose, looked at me with a tearful countenance.

'Sir,' she said, 'I place my head at your feet. Step upon it and send me to the devil's country.' She sat upon the sofa, her face darkly tearful.

'I am so ashamed to have used a worthy and kind man so ill, but I confess upon this cross and rosary' — she kissed them loudly — 'that the devil should take me if it was a deliberate act. It did show a little, but my benefactress assured me that it would pass. I was in a deep pit with the worry of it and called upon your friend for aid.'

'My friend?'

'Yes, Sir. Mr Dunbar. Is he not your friend?'

'Yes, he is.'

'He introduced me to a physician and I was four months under his hand until he pronounced me cured. Pray forgive me, Sir. It is my shame. I regret it and hope you give me leave to enquire after your health?'

'I am greatly relieved to say that I am cured also.'

She shook her head and buried her face in her hands. She was genuinely weeping.

'I am young — too young to be ravaged by such a dreadful ailment.'

I had only now found it possible to take in my surroundings: clean, neat and arranged with taste. But certainly not extravagant. I wanted to comfort her. She had suddenly become a small, helpless creature caught in the web of men's lust and intrigue. The man who gave it to her must have known that he was the bearer of bad tidings. Other things being equal, and his name known to me, I would have challenged him to a duel as was the custom on the island.

'Delvina!' I said. 'Do not weep! But it is impossible that there can in future be any…'

'I am cured, Sir. Mr Dunbar will vouch for my cure brought about with his help. He will acquaint you of the physician. For we did not deal in names. I am truly cured.'

'Dunbar is abroad. Until he returns, upon my honour I cannot associate with you even with the utmost secrecy.'

Was my need for lowlife in Bridgetown in some way the result of my life among the Caribs, whose world was confined only to that part of the bush in which they lived? Had my horizons become set like theirs upon what was within easy reach and whatever did not tax me? I had not, although removed from the forest, become what I used to be. My nature — my noble nature — had grown sadly tainted.

I bade Delvina farewell, a great pity in my heart, my desire for her a burden to me. I, however, resisted temptation and left her. As I walked down the stairs, the old woman appeared and, curtseying before me, stretched out her hand, which I contemptuously ignored. I hastened away, happy that I had repaid the bloated creature with silence for her indiscretion.

I was unable to enjoy the countryside, sullied by decrepit Irish people tending their meagre gardens, more like wasteland than cultivated land, and jabbering in their native tongue one to the other. A few of them walking in the street crossed themselves at the sight of an Englishman or a slave, both to them being devils.

As promised, I joined Sybil, Harry, Anne and a few other intimate friends for the Christmas festivities. The service we attended on the Yuletide eve was uplifting, and afterwards there was music and wassailing as though we were at home. For the slaves, who were issued rations and then left to fend for themselves, Christmas brought a time of extravagance during which plantation houses were invaded, the most unbelievable liberties taken, and cheerfully tolerated by their owners. The slaves, with rhymes and cacophonous music, danced and gyrated for the amusement of their masters, some of whom took field-hands as partners to dance with, and allowed them to make free with the refreshments. It was an unusual sight to see the close intercourse between people who were normally as far apart as it was possible to be.

Christmas was the time of the black bacchanalia. The feasting continued long into the night and often for several days, then greetings and wishes for health, wealth and prosperity exchanged, and the slaves departed for their cabins, which were always neat and clean to welcome visitors. The following day we visited Sybil's. There plays were enacted and competitions of various sorts held with the mistress adjudicating, or serving food and sharing jokes with all her people. It was a very heartening and informing season and I was further touched by the real and true goodness of these cultured English people, so tolerant of slaves who would have had no conscience about killing them if it came to that.

After much thought, I had decided to employ Delvina as my housekeeper. She, though, was greatly resented by some of the house-slaves who saw her as a meddlesome plague upon a situation that had been their own. After meeting severe resistance, Delvina relinquished the housekeeping, and the old hands once more grasped the reins. Her time was now her own. To friends, she was my servant and made a great show of it. In truth, I made no demands upon her. She commanded the freedom to come and go at will. I shunned her in private until I had got to the heart of the matter, and ascertained the truth from her physician. I was determined to resist her charms, and keep her only as a companion whose conversation I found entertaining at the end of the day.

Without ceremony, the abolitionists arrived upon the island to study the health of the slaves. Their goal, it was rumoured, was to persuade the Parliament in England to legislate for adequate provisions to be made for the care of sick slaves. The diet of the slaves, contended the abolitionists, was unnatural, consisting of salted beef, pork, rice, plantains, sugar and rum. Only a few of the slaves grew vegetables and, according to Dr Clarkson, nephew of a generation of abolitionists by the same name, their diet could and should be improved by giving them more time to grow their own produce. His wife — my Alice — piously supported him. When not thus employed, she taught the slaves the Scriptures and offered them words of consolation. They were concerned too with the Caribs, hunted by both the French and ourselves, and I was certain that the boy Tim had also been brought to Barbados to play some part in her abolitionist retinue. He was, I rapidly discovered, able to draw the most elaborate pictures upon palm and plantain leaves. The utility of this talent to the Clarksons, I was to discover later. In addition to Tim, there was Alice's personal slave, Nimbah, who had survived a mutiny of women slaves in the Gold Coast. She never failed to describe it, as twice, nay thrice, she did to me during my brief sojourn in Santa Lucia. At three different meals, her mistress had prompted, 'Now tell Mr Inkle your story and show off your excellent English, dear Nimbah.'

'Yes'm. We were taken to the deck to be of service to the sailors who had stayed behind when others had gone ashore. Three or four perhaps had stayed behind. One had carelessly left a hammer lying idle and this we found and took down to the women, who at once broke their chains with it. While some kept the drunken sailors busy, other wretched women crept up upon the sailors and began to kill them, but they managed to call upon their Dutch brethren who came to their aid with mighty guns and cutlasses, causing dead slaves to fall upon us, who were lying on the deck, for we had been stimulated with rum and made helpless. I was covered over with bodies. Oh God, sweet God, shall I be killed, robbed of air and light? But no, when they threw the bodies into the sea, I saw the light and gave a shriek and they took me up. Please spare me. Spare me! I am a mere slave. They let me live because so many of my people had died which was trouble and loss of gold to the captain. I thank you, Mr Inkle. Is not my English splendid?'

I thanked Nimbah for her story, but was forced to suffer it twice more that week.

I had intended to visit Dr and Mrs Clarkson at the Codrington plantation administered by the Society for the Propagation of the Gospel in Foreign Parts, but Dunbar, who had just returned to the island, called to give all the news from Georgia and Virginia. My brother Adam had a fine family of sons and daughters, all eager to make my acquaintance. Dunbar had visited them and they were eager that I should do so too.

Eagerly I disclosed my news of Delvina and was happy to

learn that she and I had enjoyed the services of the same physician, for which kind deed Dunbar held himself responsible, being an obliging friend of Mary Bella's.

We spent a wonderful evening, talking and drinking — for I was now able to tolerate planter's punch more securely than I had done before. It was a merry night. When I returned to my house I found Delvina walking and talking animatedly with Reginald Carey, my overseer. I was most distressed and indignantly asked her what had come upon her. She replied that he had declared his interest in her and had asked her to think how her answer would be should he ask her to be his wedded wife.

'Now, what shall I say? Do you think him a fit person to make a wife of your housekeeper?' She laughed a gargling, mocking laugh.

'It would be a sober thing to marry, although I have not yet embarked on that road.'

'Well, I will let him ask me three times, or perhaps four, and by then the answer will have formed itself into something that would be either nice or disturbing to that poor man, with the noisy eyes and the boiling heart.'

I stared at her, so small and fragile, her limbs like those of a doll that had been mostly carried by its legs, who through all her batterings by fate and the heat of Barbados, somehow managed to preserved her beauty.

'You are afraid of me, are you not? Every time I think of it, there is an agony in my poor, sinful soul. Look at the size of me. A wisp of a thing but big with evil like a woman close to her time.'

'We will not talk of that. Come. There is no harm now.'

Afterwards, though, I waited with much anxiety to see if there would be a recurrence of the gift that had caused me so much pain and anxiety. Delvina, too, was tortured by her guilt and shame, not knowing what would come, but nothing occurred for we were both truly cured thanks to Dunbar's help and the physician's skill.

After this I was a happy man, pleased in every way with my love. Dunbar had proved his friendship to me in countless ways, but his kindness in this, particular regard was worthy of brotherly love. He was in my heart where Adam and Jonathan had once been. No, I would not visit Georgia and meet more people and put a strain upon my constitution. Besides, Sir Harry and Lady Sybil were in the process of returning to Georgia where their daughter resided, and I was certain that they would convey whatever sentiments I wished to my brother and his family.

Dissension broke out on my plantation between Delvina's pets and those slaves who were favoured by my overseer, but deep in my heart I blamed the talk of freedom which was a dream of all the slaves. The very presence of the Clarksons on the islands, encouraged by their articulate brethren in London, was to be taken seriously. I did not encourage Dr Clarkson to visit our hospital or even talk to my slaves, although I had permitted Alice to come to share the Gospel message with them.

I ordered that all troublemakers who disobeyed instructions should be caged: that meant inserting them in a wooden slatted cage and starving them until they repented or died. The slaves feared this punishment greatly. One of the first I ordered to be caged was the son of my most faithful slave, who kept his distance from all trouble and kept me informed about affairs in the slave quarters. He approached me regarding the harshness of my actions. The boy, he said, had always been obedient and hardworking and had come under the eye of the overseer for his own wicked purposes. The truth of his words I found shaming. I bade him hold his tongue and when he did not I ordered the boy to be removed and arranged for him to be hanged for his father's temerity. The boy stood on a cart, the noose around his neck, and I with my own hands urged the horse to walk away to leave the boy hanging.

Later that day, Alice came to visit the slaves. When she learnt what had passed, she came to the house to seek me out.

I had not suspected that she, confident that I was a fair and lenient man, had advised the old man to approach me and plead against injustice.

Trembling with feelings of outrage, she approached me, her eyes full of tears.

'Tommy! Tommy!' she shrieked. 'You are the devil incarnate. How could you be so unjust? So coldly wicked?' She began to sob.

I approached her.

'Do not come any closer, Tommy! I must acquaint John of what occurred here. Mercifully there is the flux on a plantation to which he has been called, or he would have witnessed your cruelty. What has become of your kindly nature?'

'The lad was an insolent pup anyway,' I called after her.

'And what of the loyal old man who has been so brutally repaid for his patient service?'

'He has other sons. Don't make such scenes over a trivial happening. The impudence of slaves must be controlled. He is a slave and must serve patiently.'

She glared at me and then walked away, still sobbing and muttering some words of comfort, as she called them, from the Good Book.

The next day being Thursday, it was customary to dine with Dunbar, but he sent a messenger to inform me that there was much illness about his slaves. 'If this continues I shall certainly be ruined. We will not dine tonight.'

I thought at once of John Clarkson, who had worked among the slaves, learning their cures, and using them with success on plantations where all hope had been lost. I despatched word to him. All day the messenger searched and in the end found him on a very poor plantation in St John. I explained about the cruelty which fear of rebellion had forced upon me. Christian that he was, he willingly decided to help, for had he not sworn to alleviate human suffering? Alice and her band of Caribs and manumitted slaves accompanied him, and although several slaves had died, the flux was contained. Dunbar, grateful to the doctor, gave him the freedom of his plantation and thanked me heartily for obtaining help.

Alice was fully occupied at the Codrington estate, and for a while our paths did not cross. But I sensed the sullenness of my slaves. They greeted me without fire, as if to say, "You could kill us but you could not make us smile". Delvina seemed to be sorry, too, for the old man's loss and remained undecided about the future of her work in my household.

A letter arrived from Sybil, still in Georgia. She had regained her health but Harry, poor Harry, had died of the cold weather. I felt very sad, but death is the disease that everyone catches along life's way.

That night I dined alone. Later, however, I summoned Delvina to discuss a great increase in the household expenses. She was extremely skittish about the whole affair and sat astride my lap as she talked away. After a while I found my urges more compelling than my will and we spent that evening in the most blissful of embraces.

'Do you know,' she chirped, 'I have seen signs these three months. I am with child. Are you the father of this poor child that is growing in me? Carey is a decent Christian man and gets all he needs from the slaves. He has never once taken any liberties with my person, which is a sacred place to him, to be sure.'

'There is nothing I can do about it. Leave it here when it is born and all will be well for it. It will belong to the plantation and free of concerns.'

'Good,' she said. 'You have laid bare your heart and I understand. I wonder who *is* the father of this poor thing with its seven months of life?'

Another problem! Another visit to my friend!

'To marry her,' he said, 'would be to plunge in a sea of flotsam. She's flighty and must marry the overseer. I will keep her on my plantation or Anne will, until the child is born, then for a sizeable sum you could buy her silence or even have the slaves dismiss her. It is all so simple. Why do you panic so?'

Dismiss! I could never have seen Delvina dead. She was life! She was joy and fun and satisfaction. It would be most satisfying to see her wed! And then for a fee her husband would turn a blind eye to the nights she spent with me.

We laughed merrily and drank our coffee with ease. Dunbar was such an exceptional man, containing in his head all the solutions to life's problems. He had swum in all kinds of waters and had survived. I loved and envied his wisdom and felt the utmost tenderness to him.

We sat at breakfast until someone mentioned that a slave child, which would cost seven pounds to replace, had been severely bitten by a poisonous snake and would surely die.

'Don't you know the cure, Inkle?' voices joked. 'What did those Caribs teach you besides the pleasuring of their women? What kind of an aphrodisiac did they administer?' They meant antidote.

The jesting continued until I denied all knowledge of cures and all inclination to help and continued in the company of my friend, Dunbar. Calmed by his presence and enjoying the heartiness with which he partook of his kedgeree, I enjoyed mine also, though it irked me that there were those who still thought me tainted by my sojourn among the Caribs. I had not been a powerless hostage. I had sought at every turn to show them the superiority of my nation.

CHAPTER EIGHT

I felt quietly delighted with Delvina's news but the way I had been treated by Alice left a bad taste in my mouth. I wanted, in my own way, to teach her a lesson — surrounded though she might be by God and all His angels. I would allow her access to my slaves, encourage her activities, then with my friends reveal her trade, and shame her into leaving the island, taking her sanctimonious husband and helpers with her. I proceeded to think through a plan to achieve this end.

As usual the trade in antiquities was brisk. The French, fearing attacks from the English, and vice versa, made frequent trips to dispose of their treasures. We in the Caribbean were then at the forefront of the war between the European powers and lived in deep fear of sackings, plunder, blockades and attack. I made it known that I would be going to Martinique to buy some of the incredible articles available there. These were produced by skilled Jews, though so rife was prejudice against the Irish, Jews and slaves in Barbados, that only after articles were bought and paid for, could the craftsman be revealed as a Jew.

I despatched a letter to Alice, asking forgiveness for my cruelty and telling of my visit to Santa Lucia, and two days later ostentatiously left my plantation in a chaise with my friend, Dunbar, riding beside me. A mile or so from the house we turned round and headed back to Dunbar's house to await nightfall.

I was certain that Alice and her husband, knowing that I was away, would take opportunity to consort with my slaves, to instruct them against me and stir up strife among them. I was sure, too, that the abolitionists, with all their talk of milk and honey in heaven, had been the cause of the two suicides on my plantation.

Delvina, I learned, had gone to visit the low folk she knew in St John and would return later in the day. I had looked forward to her joining me and, without her, time hung heavily at Dunbar's. With Dunbar out rounding up some of his friends, the field-slaves away in the field, the house-slaves quietly employed in idle scheming, the silence crept all over the house like waves over sand and tree roots.

Thank God for a brief shower breaking the monotony of the familiar. Thank heaven for the sudden laughter of a slave girl and the clinking of cutlery. But the hours passed and the shadows slowly lengthened. From the bedroom I could see the sun, enigmatically red, and almost buried in a shroud of diaphanous clouds.

It grew darker and then very dark and then I heard the pounding of horses' hooves. Dunbar and some other club members, now alive to the plot, were approaching. It was our plan to expose Dr Clarkson as a spy — albeit a French spy — and thus ruin his reputation and send them from the island.

I joined them and in a greatly elated mood we rode off to my plantation. Hooves pounding, the breaths of our horses smothering the delicate sounds of night, we rode on. Not unlike the skies of the forest, this world was studded with stars that fell and turned to courting fireflies on the ground.

The shadows of the trees, like dense misshapen ogres on the land, seemed solitary but yet I mistrusted them. From the Caribs I had learned that no one is ever alone. There were always eyes — those of birds, bees, or the living, or the dead ancestors.

We dismounted and started creeping towards the plantation. It was as silent as a church after the preacher had left. We made our way to the open ground surrounded by the lignum vitae, the silk cottons and the frangipani trees. The slaves were out there listening to Delvina, who to my disgust was evidently a conspirator as well, singing one of her songs, The lights low on the ground made the shadows of the slaves large and dense. Delvina looked heavily pregnant, but still managed to accompany her own soft singing, though with softer, more restrained gestures:

> He told me soft words
> One sweet summer's day
> As to the deep woods
> We ambled away.
> He kissed me twice,
> He had his way
> And now sweet virtue has
> Gone astray.
> Oh here I stand, sad and alone,
> Cold and shivering to the bone.
> And when my child is newly born
> Of sweet virtue I will be shorn.
> He told me soft words
> One summer's day
> And to the deep woods
> We ambled away.
> He kissed me twice,
> Nay it was once
> And I became a prey to Chance.

Her poignant singing had the slaves spellbound. What did they understand about being with a deceiver on a summer's day in the woods? They understood, I was certain, the meaning of 'shivering', for that they did in the cold mornings, dressed in thin, tattered plantation rags.

Then it was Alice's turn.

'I have been told there are suicides amongst you. It is wrong to bring about your own death. It means you will never go back to your beloved Africa. It means that your ancestors will not be there to receive you, for suicide changes your features and you are not recognised by your people.'

There was a deep guttural moaning, much like the monkeys of the forest. More and louder were words of approval and promises of restraint. 'One day, perhaps when we are in heaven, your children will be free. For now, you must abide slavery. As Jesus bore his cross, so you must bear yours. No more hanging blocks of wood around your necks and swimming out to sea.'

'Oh, but it is good, Mistress. Massa Inkle does not care about us — only about chairs and tables. Massa Inkle hates people. He has much evil inside his belly, his heart, and his head.'

I started forward.

'Don't,' whispered Dunbar. 'Let Clarkson speak. His wife has done no harm so far!'

Clarkson came forward.

'Eat the vegetables you grow. Whatever happens, grow vegetables and eat them though they are strange. You must keep up your strength and health. Do not disobey your masters, and be careful of your overseers, even though they are not always worthy men. What will happen to you is in God's hands. We can all pray for better times. You must keep your courage up and God will help you. Now, some of your men and women have been very brave and they have received God's blessing. Nimbah here will tell you her story.'

Nimbah, her head covered with paper bows, once again told her story in impeccable English.

Then Kwashiba told of how she had given birth to twins. 'My husband thought that the devil was the father of one but he could not say which, for they were both boys. We were all to be killed. My master saved me. He told my husband that all four of us must die. God spoke to my husband and now we are all alive!'

The Caribs began to tell of their capture and enslavement and of their conversion to Christianity. Then a woman, strange and cadaverous, appeared.

'The Spirit Woman!' hissed Dunbar. 'She tells some story about how she had saved a Frenchman and he was untrue to her! He married another, but then she too finds Jesus.'

She seemed familiar but too old and broken to be Yarico. They called her Rabiel and Carib Tim translated as she spoke. Yarico knew English — some English. This could not be her?

Then Clarkson spoke again. 'Those of you who have been beaten, draw pictures of your wounds on plantain leaves with charcoal, but first smooth them with a hot stone before you draw and let Tim bring all to me. Our friends in England want to have sight of them and weep with you. The Planters will not crack like brittle wood. They are rich and strong. Some are friends of the chiefs of our country, but we have friends, too…'

This was enough proof for Dunbar, and he called out, 'Come on!' as he rushed in and grabbed Clarkson. I grabbed Alice. My hatred of her sanctimonious airs had turned into a fierce desire for her. I dragged her along the path, past the tethered horses. She began to protest, to reason with me.

'You have always been gentle. Where did this shameful unmanliness overtake you? Do not treat me so!'

My mind was set in a harsh silence and, intent upon teaching her a lesson, I dragged her into my house. She continued shrieking and calling upon God to save her from my devilish intentions, whilst I replied that God had saved me from her folly.

What happened to Clarkson, Delvina, her intended, and some of the slaves, I was to be told later. I concentrated on Alice — prim, proper, dressed in clothes as if in armour. What was she hiding? I had roamed around the forest dressed in paint for seven long years. I plunged my hand into the neck of her dress and ripped it away from her. I was conscious only of the angry rip and tear of fabric. I was shredding her clothes as we ripped the leaves off the forest trees. She screamed.

'I will teach you piety,' I snarled. 'I wanted you, waited for you, dreamt of you and now what are you doing? Loving savages as I was forced to do.'

'Please! Contain yourself, contain yourself or you will surely rue the day. Tim! Tim! Don't use that evil thing! Run! Run! Tim, get help! The devil in Mr Inkle has come alive!'

'You want to be a martyr? To die defending your virtue!

You will not succeed! I am the devil.' My laughter was even more menacing in the darkness.

She looked ridiculous in tatters, her pink skin contrasting with the strips of patterned fabric. I was calm now, but mad with desire and hatred of her. I began carefully to remove what was left of her torn clothes, deliberately scratching her with my nails. I would have my way. I would... I would. As I struggled with my own apparel, while trying to subdue her, I felt a sudden sting upon my leg. Briefly conscious of the dart in my leg I began to disappear from myself. I heard no more. My world was turning round and round, moving from light to darker and darker darkness.

When I came to, the physician who had attended me previously was with me and I was confined in a straitjacket.

'Mr Inkle, you went too far, much too far. It was a most shameful performance!'

'And Mrs Clarkson?' I asked, shame, scalding me like boiling water. 'Did she suffer violence?'

'No. You were prevented. She was terrified, shaken and angry. She said that you were possessed. She prays that you will be spiritually rebuilt. Dr Clarkson, poor man, is, however, still badly hurt from the beating he received. Your leg has been poisoned and had it not been for the efforts of the Spirit Woman, who knew the antidote to the poison used by the Carib boy, I can assure you, Mr Inkle, you would have been no more.'

'Why did the boy want to hurt me? I never hurt him.'

'He loved his mistress, and must with his weapons defend her life. He is also certain, and swore to it, that in another life you poisoned his friend called Waiyo. Did you know anyone by that name? He claims he let white men remove him from his tribe so that he could find you,' he said. 'The oracle stones led him to you.'

Like Peter, I denied Christ! So Toru, now Tim, had come! Silence hung about like hard frost but I had to speak.

'No,' I said bending my tongue. 'I am sure he was mistaken. I never knew a man called Waiyo. I did not! Never!'

Then I muttered, as if calling up a ghost, 'Waiyo… I did not know him. Tim is mistaken.'

'He says he recognised you by the tattoo you wear. He saw it as you slept. It is the condor of the forest Caribs. The woman, Rabiel, comes from the same tribe. She was saved from the sea but was so famished and distracted that she lost her mind — exchanged it with the sea spirits for her life, as she puts it.'

'Where is the woman now?'

'I don't know, but she promised she would come when you are asleep and dress your wounds. I will call again later. There are many mysteries here.'

I lay in my bed, moving in and out of consciousness, sleep, dreams and nightmares. Shame and resentment battled for dominion. At times I felt quite unrepentant over my treatment of Alice. I had looked forward to a reunion with her, to pick up the pieces of my old life and I had been foiled. She was responsible for my present state. I had no wife and no heir. I had arrived in the present dressed in my father's clothes, speaking in his voice and selling his antiquities. Alice's husband was plain humbug, yet he had his place in the service of humanity. What of me? And Alice, what of her? Scared of love and motherhood? I hated life. The sight of the sun and the clear blue skies nauseated me.

I must have fallen asleep only lightly, for I was suddenly conscious of the Spirit Woman changing the poultice on my wound.

'Yarico!' I called softly. 'Yarico! Is it you? I am happy you did not perish. The forest always reclaims its own. Speak, if you are Yarico.'

She worked away unheeding, her hands shining like glass in the sunshine.

'Rabiel!' I called again.

'They will come! They will come!' I heard once more.

It came as if through a thunderstorm of years. Once more I saw Yarico drown our child. I wept for all those moments when I did not weep.

As my strength gradually returned, I felt an irresistible urge to get up out of my bed and walk. I needed to escape from this stifling room where I struggled with the demons in my mind. I was sitting on the edge of the bed, dizzy with the effort, when the physician arrived.

'You will need either crutches or a stick,' he warned. 'There is no strengthening that leg. There never will be. You will never walk unaided again. Be thankful that your leg has not been amputated.'

'Oh God. Am I a cripple?'

'Near enough,' said the physician.

I reached down and felt for my foot. It was without feeling.

'Then I will have to find Delvina. She alone will be able to take care of me and love me as a woman should.'

He gave me a strange look which said many things. As he poured me a drink, I heard voices outside. They seemed to be in eager conversation. Dunbar and Anne entered. She carried a small bouquet of roses. Slaves followed with baskets of fruit and flowers.

'How are you, my good man?' asked Dunbar. 'I hope to see you in radiant health in the shortest possible time.'

'Yes, yes!' I replied irritably. 'Have the abolitionists fled?'

'No. They are under the protection of the King's representative. But Clarkson is still sick and his wife actively tender in his recovery.'

'And Delvina? I want her here to tend me.'

'Well, old fellow, I think you should…'

'Dead!' said Anne. 'Delvina is dead.'

'Dead?' I asked, stunned. 'How so? Where has she gone?'

'She gave birth and died.'

'And the child?'

'She presented him to Alice as she was dying. Her last words were, "Keep him from Inkle. Keep him and call him Christian".'

'He is my son.'

'He is not your son! He was given by the mother to the Clarksons. He is theirs.'

'How did she die?'

'One of our people cut her with his whip and the shock of it forced her time and she died. We were too headstrong in our urge to overcome them. We helped their cause and damaged our own. There will be much sympathy for them in England.'

'She was sunshine and showers.'

'Who was?' Dunbar asked.

'And dew beads and flowers,' I continued.

'What are you talking about?'

'Yarico, Zeze and Delvina. All of them,' I said dully.

'Who was Yarico?' asked Anne.

'My Carib wife.'

'And Zeze?'

'My slave lover. You know who Delvina was.'

At the mention of her name, uncontrollable pain racked my body and I once more wept unashamedly. At that moment I renounced my stiff upper lip, my self-control. I became a man who felt loss, sorrow and deep anguish. With Delvina I was able to be young again, share in fantasy and act out my life among the Caribs. Nudity did not agitate her. With her, the body was an instrument of pleasure like the violin or the flute. Sometimes she played as if music was written for it. Allegro or andante, she played. At other times she played according to touch and sentiment.

I wept and Anne, in an effort to console, said, 'Tommy, you were enslaved! You married one of your captors!'

'Yes, Anne.' I nodded in confirmation.

'It was not a vile rumour?'

'No, I married. We had two children. And if I am cursed to be a cripple, no one will be able to save me. I am a sinful man!'

No one spoke for a considerable time.

'Did you know Inkle's secret, Mr. Dunbar?' Anne asked timidly.

'I did know,' admitted Dunbar. 'I was with him the day he sold her. He needed money and she did not seem to mind being sold. Perhaps she did… she threw…'

'No more of the past. We must carry on and never forfeit

136

the future,' said Anne, her charming face encircled by the froth of her bonnet.

I took her hand and kissed it.

'Would you marry a cripple, Anne?'

'I don't know,' she said. 'I shall have to examine you as the slaves are examined before purchase.' She gave a little chuckle and I smiled at her.

Delvina's funeral brought the whole island together. Planters attended out of courtesy to Mary Bella, wives out of regard for their husbands, slaves out of love of a childlike mistress, and fellow courtesans because they admired her frank, many-sided nature. Anne went because I could not bring myself to go. She reported that the Clarksons were both present, with Bibles, flowers, and little Christian. I learned too that the Caribs had stood behind bushes and shrubs as the cortège passed by. And Carib Tim carried his blowpipe, just in case he had need of it.

As I sat in a stupor of reflection, my past a beacon in my mind's eye, I could not help wondering about his future, as the abolitionists would certainly civilise him, causing him to lose his traditions and his skills. For an instant, the thought to adopt him and return him to his nation crossed my mind, but I stifled it, believing that he would surely return to his people in his own good time and in his own manner.

Life on my estate resumed its routines. The Clarksons re-turned to England with Christian, and for a time the rumours about imminent abolition died. I remained convinced that slavery must be preserved, though conducted as humanely as possible. There were times when I wished to sell my planta-tion and have done with it all, but when my slaves expressed their unhappiness at the thought of passing into the hands of a master yet unknown, (for they were simply a part of the stock and would be sold too) I deferred my decision. One day, after I had admonished an overseer for some unmerited act of brutality, Anne had laughingly said, 'The Devil made overse-ers and God made us.'

'And who made the Indians?'

'I cannot guess. But Columbus said in his report to Ferdinand and Isabella, "So lovable, so tractable, so peaceable are these people that I swear to Your Majesties that there is not in the world a better nation or a better land. They love their neighbours as themselves and their discourse is ever sweet and gentle and accompanied with a smile".'

'Or with a blowpipe,' I added. 'They are a great people when one thinks without prejudice about them.'

The years came round without event, until one year, my friend Dunbar, who had made money effortlessly and spent it in the same manner, packed up his business in Barbados and boarded one of his own ships to return to his home plantation in Virginia. I bade him goodbye with a deep sense of foreboding, for there was much piracy, attack from both French and Spanish privateers and maraudings on the high seas. He epitomised all that was English and all that made our nation worthy of renown. Weeks later, we were hugely sad to learn that the ship had foundered on some rocks and lost with all hands. When I think of him, I believe that should I get to Heaven, our natural home, he will be present there with friendship, understanding, advice and good service, which he offered here on Earth. I sigh at his memory, and say, 'I have lost a dear friend' and to thoughts of those others, Yarico, Zeze, Chief Tomo, and Delvina I say, 'I have lost those I once knew in whole and in part.'

I have set down the full story of my life among the Caribs. Make what you will of it, gentle reader, for the truth burns like fire and chills like ice. And nature is both ice and fire — neither one or the other.

Today, I hold no doubt in my heart. I have enjoyed all that could be purchased with wealth. I have gained solace from marriage to a wife who had an aristocratic poise and a simple, endearing manner, and with whom I relieved myself of a great burden and found peace of mind. With her, long after   I escaped from the Black Caribs, my fragmented mind was made whole. And Yarico? Well, she is the spirit of the woods and all that is good and green in Nature; returning and flourishing in the rain, sparkling in the dew, and melting in the blue of the skies and the beaded darkness of the night.

But I must never think of love when I recall our life together. I must think of mystery, and the articulate formations of shadows and sunlight in the forest. There is nothing illicit about the forest. There is only encumbrance and encroachment of one thing upon another. The members of a tribe live as though one heart beats for all. That was difficult for me to learn for I am a man who believes that our civilisation is superior and permanent. I hold all others to be ephemeral — and at times grotesque. That is our way as a nation.

Many years have passed since we left the island of Barbados, thus named from the tribe of bearded Indians who lived there in earlier centuries. The cause of abolition grows apace. As a leading anti-abolitionist I travel the length and breadth of England to acquaint the populace of the futility of setting natives free, thus reducing the amount of sugar in our tea and gold in our coffers. To be sure, my incapacity has proved a boon, for it is blamed, without any help from me, upon the barbarity of savages, who should be kept chained and set to work.

Poor Anne died of age during her mid-morning slumber. She truly loved her nation. My pain at her death was sharper than the thrust of a thousand swords but it subsided and the fondest of memories now occupy a place in my heart. She and Alice were facets of my country, loyalty, honour, conviction and patriotism. And each sang the songs I knew and loved in the green oasis of my youth. I bless them both and pray that a merciful God will hear my fervent prayers and nurture and guard my Anne in the gardens of Paradise. As for Yarico, what is she now in my scheme of things? I cannot tell! I cannot tell!

AFTERWORD

The narrative of Inkle and Yarico, originating in Ligon's history of Barbados, appeared in a number of seventeenth and eighteenth century versions, including a play by George Coleman. The version included below was written by Richard Steele and appeared in the *Spectator* (No. 11, Tuesday, March 13, 1711).

I was the other Day amusing my self with *Ligon's* Account of *Barbadoes*; and, in Answer to your well-wrought Tale, I will give you (as it dwells upon my memory) out of that honest traveller, in his fifty-fifth Page, the history of *Inkle* and *Yarico*.

 Mr. *Thomas Inkle*, of London, aged twenty Years, embarked in the *Downs* on the good Ship called the *Achilles*, bound for the *West-Indies*, on the 16th of June, 1647, in order to improve his fortune by trade and merchandize. Our adventurer was the third son of an eminent citizen, who had taken particular care to instill into his mind an early love of gain, by making him a perfect master of numbers, and consequently giving him a *quick* view of loss and advantage, and preventing the natural impulses of his passions, by prepossession towards his interests. With a mind thus turned, young *Inkle* had a person every way agreeable, a ruddy vigour in his countenance, strength in his limbs, ringlets of fair hair loosely flowing on his shoulders. It happened in the course of the voyage, that the *Achilles*, in some distress, put into a creek on the main of *America*, in search of provisions: the youth, who is the hero of my story, among others, went ashore on this occasion. From their first landing they were observed by a party of *Indians*, who hid themselves in the woods for that purpose. The *English* unadvisedly marched a great distance from the shore into the country, and were intercepted by the natives, who slew the greatest number of them. Our adventurer escaped among others, by flying into a forest. Upon his coming into a remote and pathless part of the wood, he threw himself, tired and breathless, on a little hillock, when an *Indian* maid rushed from a thicket behind him; after the first surprize, they appeared mutually agreeable to each other. If the *European* was highly charmed with the limbs, features, and wild graces of the naked *American*; the *American* was no less taken with the dress, complexion, and shape of an *European*, covered from head to foot. The *Indian* grew immediately enamoured of him, and consequently sollicitous for his preservation: she therefore conveyed him to a cave, where she gave him a delicious repast of fruits, and led him to a stream to slake his thirst. In the midst of these good offices, she would sometimes play with his hair, and delight in the opposition of its colour to that of her fingers; then open his bosom, then laugh at him for covering it. She was, it seems, a person of distinction, for she every day came to him in a different dress, of the most beautiful shells, bugles, and bredes. She likewise brought him a great many spoils, which her other Lovers had presented to her, so that his cave was richly adorned with all the spotted skins of beasts, and most party-coloured feathers of fowls, which that world afforded. To make his confinement more tolerable, she would carry him in the dusk of the evening, or by the favour of moonlight, to unfrequented groves and solitudes, and shew him where to lye down in safety and sleep amidst the falls of waters, and melody of nightingales. Her part was to watch and hold him awake in her arms, for fear of her countrymen, and awake him on occasions to consult his safety. In this manner did the lovers pass away their time, till they had learn'd a language of their own, in which the voyager communicated to his mistress, how happy he should be to have her in his country, where she should be cloathed in such silks as his wastecoat was made of, and be carried in houses drawn by horses, without being exposed to wind or weather. All this he promised her the enjoyment of, without such fears and alarms as they were there tormented with. In this tender Correspondence these lovers lived for several months, when *Yarico*, instructed by her lover, discovered a vessel on the coast, to which she made signals; and in the night, with the utmost joy and satisfaction, accompanied him to a ship's-crew of his countrymen, bound for *Barbadoes*. When a vessel from the main arrives in that island, it seems the planters come down to the shoar, where there is an immediate market of the *Indians* and other slaves, as with us of horses and oxen.

To be short, Mr. *Thomas Inkle*, now coming into English territories, began seriously to reflect upon his loss of time, and to weigh with himself how many days interest of his money he had lost during his stay with *Yarico*. This thought made the young man very pensive, and careful what account he should be able to give his friends of his voyage. Upon which considerations, the prudent and frugal young man sold Yarico to a Barbadian merchant; notwithstanding that the poor girl, to incline him to commiserate her condition, told him that she was with child by him; But he only made use of that information, to rise in his demands upon the purchaser.

I was so touch'd with this story, (which I think should be always a counterpart to the *Ephesian* matron) that I left the room with tears in my eyes; which a woman of *Arietta's* good sense, did, I am sure, take for greater applause than any compliments I could make her.

Publisher's Note

Since Beryl Gilroy's novel was first published, the publication of Frank Felstenstein's *English Trader; Indian Maid: A Inkle and Yarico Reader* (Maryland: The Johns Hopkins University Press, 1999) has provided an extensive survey of versions of the narrative between Ligon's of 1657 and a Barbadian version of 1840.

Beryl Agatha Gilroy (nee Alnwich) was born on 30 August, 1924 in Skeldon village, in Berbice County in British Guiana. She grew up in a large, extended family, largely under the influence of her maternal grandmother, Sally Louisa James (1868-1967), a herbalist, manager of the family smallholding, keen reader, imparter to the young Beryl of the stories of Long Bubbies, Cabresses and Long Lady and a treasury of colloquial proverbs. Her grandmother also took the view that the child would learn more by being taken all over the county with her, and being given space for wonder and enquiry, than in the regimented system of primary schooling. As a result Beryl Gilroy did not enter full time schooling until she was twelve. It is clear that much of her grandmother's influence persisted in Beryl Gilroy's own philosophy of education (she educated her own children at home) that stressed freedom for discovery within a framework of basic skills. She recalls the importance of the gift her grandfather gave her of a dictionary after suffering the humiliation of laughter over some childish misuse of a word. Her grandmother also taught that people should avoid 'spirit poorness' (victimhood) and this philosophy permeates all Beryl Gilroy's writing. The experiences of this Berbician childhood are told, above all, in *Sunlight on Sweet Water* (Peepal Tree, 1994).

More formal education followed and Beryl Gilroy, awarded a British Guiana Teacher's Certificate with first class honours, worked as a school teacher in Guyana until 1951 when at the age of 27 she was selected to attend university in the United Kingdom. Between 1951-53 she attended the University of London pursuing a Diploma in Child Development. Although a qualified teacher, racism prevented her getting a post for some time, and she had to work as a washer-up at Lyons, a factory clerk and lady's maid. She taught for a couple of years, married (one of the earliest interracial marriages in the post-war period) and spent the next twelve years at home bringing up/educating her children, furthering her own higher education, reviewing and reading for a publisher. In 1968 she returned to teaching and eventually became probably the first Black headteacher in the UK. Her experiences of those years are told in *Black Teacher* (1976). Later she worked as a researcher at the University of London and developed a pioneering practice in psychotherapy, working mainly with Black women and children.

Her own creative writing began in childhood, as a teacher for children and then in the 1960s when she began writing what was later published by Peepal Tree as *In Praise of Love and Children*, sent to numerous publishers at that time but not accepted as 'too psychological'. However, between 1970-75 she wrote the pioneering children's series Nippers which contain probably the first reflection of the Black British presence in UK writing for children. But as a home-based person in North London suburbia, cut off from the networks of the male dominated London Caribbean writing fraternity and later from groups such as CAM (Caribbean Artists Movement), it was not until 1986 that her first novel, the award winning *Frangipani House* was published (Heinemann). (It won a GLC Creative Writing Prize in 1982). Set in an old person's home in Guyana, it reflects one of her professional concerns: the position of ethnic minority elders and her persistent emphasis on the drive for human freedom. *Boy Sandwich* (also Heinemann) was published in 1989, followed by *Steadman and Joanna: A Love in Bondage* (Vantage, 1991), and a collection of poems, *Echoes and Voices* (Vantage, 1991). Then came *Sunlight and Sweet Water* (Peepal Tree, 1994), *Gather the Faces*, *In Praise of Love and Children* and *Inkle and Yarico* (all Peepal Tree, 1994). Her last novel, *The Green Grass Tango* (Peepal Tree) was published in 2001, sadly after Beryl Gilroy's death in April of that year.

Beryl Gilroy was awarded an Honorary Doctorate by the University of London and an Honorary Fellowship by the

Institute of Education for her writing and pioneering work as a psychotherapist.

Beryl's death caused a silence on Peepal Tree's phone line that was a painful absence. She rang us regularly, to encourage, sometimes to berate, to talk about the often delayed publishing of her books in progress, and sometimes just to talk. She was like a mother to us. We missed her badly.

Sunlight on Sweet Water

ISBN: 9780948833649; pp. 139; pub. 1994; price: £7.99

Beryl Gilroy transports the reader back to the Guyanese village of her childhood to meet such characters as Mr Dewsbury the Dog Doctor, Mama Darlin' the village midwife and Mr Cumberbatch the Chief Mourner.

It was a time when 'children did not have open access to the world of adults and childhood had not yet disappeared'. Perhaps for this reason, the men and women who pass through these stories have a mystery and singularity which are as unforgettable for the reader as they were for the child. Beryl Gilroy brings back to life a whole, rich Afro-Guyanese community, where there were old people who had been the children of slaves and where Africa was not forgotten.

Sunlight on Sweet Water has long been one of Peepal Tree's best loved books and has been widely taught on women's and Caribbean literature courses.

Gather the Faces

ISBN: 9780948833885; pp. 120; pub. 1996; *price: £7.99*

Marvella Payne is twenty-seven, works as a secretary for British Rail and has pledged to the congregation of the Church of the Holy Spirit that she will abstain from sex before marriage. When she repulses the groping hands of the trainee-deacon, Carlton Springle, she resigns herself to growing old with her mother, father and Bible-soaked aunts. But Aunt Julie has other ideas and finds Marvella a penfriend from her native Guyana. When good fortune allows the couple to meet, Marvella awakens to new possibilities as she realises how bound she has been by the voices of her dependent, cossetted childhood. But will marriage be another entrapment, another loss of self?

Mary Conde writes: 'Gather the Faces is essentially the story of Marvella's redefinition of herself in relation to her friends, her family and her native Guyana. Its great triumph is in its language, in such observations as "... when one of my uncles got married, it took off his spirit like a jacket," and "Faith had returned with its feather duster." It is an entertaining, tender and moving story.'

Phyllis Briggs-Emmanuel writes in *The Caribbean Writer*: 'Gather the Faces has a happy ending and is written with Gilroy's characteristic clarity of description and fluency of language. Its optimism shimmers, its spirituality glows in the beautiful verses quoted from the Biblical Song of Songs, and the reader is revivified as faith in love is restored.'

In Praise of Love and Children
ISBN: 9780948833892; pp. 153; pub. 1996; price: £8.99

After false starts in teaching and social work, Melda Hayley finds her mission in fostering the damaged children of the first generation of black settlers in a deeply racist Britain. But though Melda finds daily uplift in her work, her inner life starts to come apart. Her brother Arnie has married a white woman and his defection from the family and the distress Melda witnesses in the children she fosters causes her own buried wounds to weep. Melda confronts the cruelties she has suffered as the 'outside child' at the hands of her stepmother. But though the past drives Melda towards breakdown, she finds strengths there too, especially in the memories of the loving, supporting women of the yards. And there is Pa who, in his new material security in the USA, discovers a gentle caring side and teaches his family to sing in praise of love and children.

Adele Newson writes in *World Literature Today*: 'Gilroy's novel hails from the tradition that celebrates community rather than the individual. Traditions are insular in spite of cultural disruptions. This is clearly marked by comparisons of culture throughout the novel. As Melda observes: "People came to the Caribbean for holidays, but we went nowhere except to family parties, excursions and funerals for ours. Talk and song were holidays to us. We believed, as the old folk had done, that it was better to be bitten by your own bedbugs than those from the beds of others." *In Praise of Love and Children* is a celebration of culture, traditions, and change. It is painful in its confrontations while liberating in its veracity to human nature.'

The Green Grass Tango
ISBN: 9781900715478; pp. 144; pub. 2001; price: £8.99

When Alfred Grayson, a retired and recently widowed civil servant, decides to buy a dog, Sheba gives him a passport to the diverse multiracial community of dog-walkers and bench-sitters who meet in a down-at-heel London park. Here Grayson engages with the cunning Finbar, theatrical Arabella and her absurd tango-dancing sidekick, Harold Heyhoe, Jamaican Maryanne, tortured by her demons, Rastafarian Rootsman, old Uncle Nat from Sierra Leone, tattooed Judy and abandoned Lucy.

Grayson, originally from Barbados, has passed for white and kept his origins quiet during his civil service career, but two, in particular, of the relationships he makes in the park cause him to rethink his past.

In the park, characters, who would not otherwise meet, make unlikely alliances and feel able to expose various identities, or in Alfred's case begin to reconstruct one. Both park and characters have their times of wintry bleakness, shabbiness and moments of glorious display. For Alfred and Lucy there is even the hope that late flowering lust might bloom into love. Like all the best, the richest and most truthful comedy, *The Green Grass Tango* is filled with a sense of human fragility and impermanence.

And there are the dogs: faithful companions and quizzical witnesses to their owners' most intimate deeds!

All 300+ Peepal Tree titles are available from the website
www.peepaltreepress.com
with a money back guarantee, secure credit card ordering
and fast delivery throughout the world at cost or less.

Peepal Tree Press is celebrated as the home of challenging
and inspiring literature from the Caribbean and Black
Britain. Visit www.peepaltreepress.com to read sample
poems and reviews, discover new authors, established
names and access a wealth of information. Subscribe to our
mailing list for news of new books and events.

Contact us at:
Peepal Tree Press, 17 King's Avenue, Leeds LS6 1QS, UK
Tel: +44 (0) 113 2451703 E-mail:
contact@peepaltreepress.com